I0530768

Bride of Pretense

Brides by Mail Series Book 1

By

Cami Wesley & Amanda Tru

Published by

Walker Hammond Publishers

Walker Hammond

Publishers

PUBLISHED BY: Walker Hammond Publishers

Some scripture quotations courtesy of the 1611 King James Version (KJV) of the Holy Bible.

Some scripture quotations courtesy of the New King James Version (NKJV) of the Holy Bible, Copyright© 1979, 1980, 1982 by Thomas-Nelson, Inc. Used by permission. All rights reserved.

Original Cover Art by Debi Warford (www.debiwarford.com)

Library Cataloging Data

Tru, Amanda (Amanda Tru) 1978-
Wesley, Cami (Cami Wesley) 1981-
    Bride of Pretense/Cami Wesley and Amanda Tru
        170 p. 20.32cm x 12.7cm (8in x 5in.)

Summary: Stealing a groom is not for the faint of heart.... or the hapless Adelaide Delaney!

Identifiers: 978-1-68190-014-8 (Trade Paperback); 978-1-68190-015-5 (POD) ; 978-1-68190-013-1 (ebook)

1. Western 2. Mail Order Bride 3. Traditional Romance 4. male and female relationships 5. Christian Inspiration

[PS3568.AW475 M328 2015]
248.8'43 — dc211

Bride of Pretense

Brides by Mail Series Book 1

By

Cami Wesley
& Amanda Tru

Table of Contents

Dedication

For Janna –

Growing up, our mother told us to be kind to your sisters because they will be your very best friends when you grow up. She was right.

You are the creamy filling in our Oreo cookie. You are what makes our trio interesting. We love you, Miz!

 *Chapter 1*

St. Louis, Missouri, 1880

ADELAIDE Delaney set her brown floral carpet bag on the bench beside her, hoping it would warn others away. The last thing she needed right now was for some overly friendly person to sit next to her, forcing a conversation.

Having the train delayed was a bad omen. Not that she needed another reason *not* to get on board.

"You don't mind if I sit here, do you?"

Addie was just about to say, yes, I definitely do mind, when the lady lowered herself onto the bench, shoving Addie's bag into her hip.

Addie tried to scoot as far away as possible, but the edge

of the bag still bit through her layers of skirts. However, the young woman next to her didn't seem to mind that half of her posterior was positioned atop Addie's carpet bag. Instead, she proceeded to take off her hat and begin fanning herself in the most unladylike fashion.

"It's so hot here, in St. Louis, isn't it?" Not waiting for a response, the woman continued. "Although, I'm from Georgia, where it's even hotter and more humid. Where are you from? I'm Charlotte, by the way. Charlotte Mason from Atlanta, Georgia. What's your name?"

Addie glowered at the young woman seated next to her, or rather on top of her bag. Addie reached between them and grabbed the small leather handles pulling them toward her, away from her unwanted companion. With a solid yank, the bag flew out and hit Addie right on her face.

"I'm so sorry!" Here, let me take your bag for you. There's plenty of room for it under the bench next to mine. There. Now you don't have to hold it. How's your nose?"

"Fine."

Addie turned away from the other girl and took out her handkerchief to delicately dab at her injured nose. Hopefully, Charlotte would take the hint, and refrain from further conversation.

But luck was not with Addie today. Charlotte continued her monologue, not seeming to notice Addie's sideways glares.

"I'm headed to Texas this afternoon to meet my fiancé." Charlotte glanced around discretely before lowering her voice in a conspiratorial whisper. "I haven't actually met him before. I'm a mail order bride."

Addie gaped at Charlotte in surprise. "Wh-what?" Oh, if

her tutor, Miss Carrington could hear Addie now! She would be horrified by her former student's uncultured stuttering. Addie was the daughter of Moses Delaney, the great shipping magnate. She did not stutter.

"Well, I saw an advertisement in the newspaper for a gentleman looking for a bride. He was very specific, saying that she had to be a good Christian girl who could cook, clean, and help with other aspects of farm life. He also required references, which I provided before we began to write letters. His name is Joshua Harding. Isn't that a handsome name?"

Charlotte once again didn't pause for an answer. "He owns a cattle ranch by Austin. He also has pigs, chickens, and a few horses. He doesn't live too close to the nearest town, about an hour's ride, which doesn't bother me because we will have each other, and we got along so wonderfully in our letters. He's simply perfect."

Charlotte paused, her blue eyes gazing off into the distance, a happy smile on her angelic face. She really did resemble an angel with her light blonde hair framing her round face and pale blue eyes. Addie had blonde hair and blue eyes too, but she looked considerably less heavenly.

"What about your family? How do they feel about you leaving your home and moving so far away to marry a stranger?"

A dark shadow passed over Charlotte's face. "I have no family. My pa died when I was little, and Mama just passed away. This is my chance to start over, to belong to someone, and have a family of my own."

"I'm so sorry." Addie regretted inadvertently bringing up a painful subject for Charlotte. Though it seemed the two women shared little in common, Addie knew what it was like to lose someone.

"Don't be," Charlotte said, her smile gently returning. "I know my family is in heaven. I also know that God is providing a new family for me."

"How can you be so sure?" Addie asked, curious in spite of herself. Charlotte seemed so certain, so confident that the train would take her to where she was meant to be. "You've never met this man. How can you know this is what you should do?"

"God told me," Charlotte replied simply.

And with those three little words, Addie immediately disliked Charlotte Mason from Georgia.

Addie held her breath, waiting for Charlotte to continue, to explain what she had meant. But with a serene smile fixed on her face, she now chose to be silent.

Addie clenched the handkerchief in her hand, trying to manage her annoyance. After sitting in the same pew, in the same church, every Sunday for her entire life, Addie had never felt that God had spoken to her directly. Most of the time, she felt like she was pushed around in the dark, sending up prayers that never reached higher than the ceiling. People like Charlotte, who seemed to have everything figured out and confidently "heard" from God, drew her instant dislike.

Not that Addie should esteem Charlotte. She wasn't exactly of the class with which Addie normally associated. Charlotte's simple brown traveling suit starkly contrasted Addie's elaborate navy one.

Addie reached up and adjusted her hat just a little. It was the newest style and just purchased for this trip. But even the physical reminder of her wealth did nothing to convince Addie that Charlotte didn't have something she longed for.

Finally, unable to take the silence any longer, Addie burst out. "I don't understand when you say, "God told you...""

Charlotte pursed her lips, as if thinking, then finally broke her silence. "Everything happens for a reason. We might not understand God's plan, but He is still in control. You have to go where God leads you, and He will take care of the rest."

"Yes, but how did you know?"

"Well, I prayed and th–" three short blasts from the train halted Charlotte's words. "Oh, no, that's my train! I really want to answer your questions, I sincerely do, I just need to freshen up before boarding. Wait here, and we will talk until I have to leave."

"But..." Addie was so close to getting her answers! Charlotte couldn't leave now! But there she was, bending to search with her fingers for the handles of a carpet bag that looked remarkably familiar.

"Wait!" Addie called, but Charlotte had already disappeared behind the depot doors. Addie glanced under the bench, confirming her suspicions. Charlotte had grabbed Addie's bag by mistake. The carpet bags were similar size and color, Addie could see how in Charlotte's haste she had taken the wrong one. Oh, well, Charlotte would be back soon, and Addie could remedy the situation before Charlotte left for Texas. Addie's train would not be leaving for another hour. She had time to wait.

Addie tapped her pointed boot to the rhythm of seconds ticking by. She stared at the impostor carpet bag beside her, wishing its owner would appear to retrieve it. To Addie, it was almost repulsive. Charlotte's bag looked like a fifty year old version of her own. The attractive brown floral pattern had faded to a muddy swirl, and both the handle and brass clasp looked as if a stiff wind could convince them to abandon their posts.

As the minutes wore on, Addie couldn't tolerate sitting still. Finally, she stood from the bench, snatched the carpet bag handle in her sweaty palm, and walked across the platform toward Charlotte's train. Stopping in the middle of the platform, she turned a full circle, craning her neck in a completely improper fashion, desperately looking for any sign of the missing mail order bride.

The train whistle blew. Startled, Addie jumped, jerking the handle of the carpet bag up sharply. The fragile brass clasp popped open. Addie tried to grab the bag before it upturned, but she only got hold of one side. With the weight of the bag shifting, it teetered. Addie reached for the other end, but couldn't grab it before the entire contents of Charlotte's bag emptied in a flood all over the train platform.

Addie gasped, immediately turning a brilliant shade of crimson at the sight of lady's undergarments spilling around her feet. She quickly bent over, trying to both hide her face and shove Charlotte's possessions back in the bag.

Mens' boots clomped their way across the platform as Addie hurriedly worked. She carefully kept her eyes down to the wayward possessions and the passing feet, never having the nerve to look up at the faces belonging to those shoes, and hoping no one would offer to help.

She stuffed the undergarments in first, followed by Charlotte's now dusty nightgown and night cap. A dress, equally brown and drab as the one Charlotte had been wearing, went in next. A tin of crackers (very likely now crumbs), a still-intact mirror, a sewing kit, and a few other small toiletries were unceremoniously returned to their home. Finally, Addie grabbed Charlotte's heavy Bible and placed it as the crown atop the other possessions.

She started to rise, but then saw a packet of envelopes hiding partially under her skirt. Addie retrieved the papers, intending to toss them on top the Bible, but at the sight of the return address, Last Chance, Texas, she paused.

These were Charlotte's letters from her would-be groom!

Without conscious thought, Addie secured the flimsy carpet bag clasp as best she could and wandered back to the bench, where she sat and stared at the packet in her hands.

Feeling a little guilty, but assuring herself that she would only look to see if Charlotte's train ticket was amongst the papers, Addie undid the neatly tied cornflower blue ribbon binding the envelopes together. Thumbing through, Addie found the ticket at the very back, where Charlotte had obviously slid it in to keep it safe.

Instead of re-tying the ribbon and replacing the letters in the bag, Addie leafed back through the envelopes, noting that Charlotte's Joshua Harding had a very strong, masculine scrawl.

Now feeling a lot more guilty, Addie watched as her slightly trembling fingers slid out the papers folded neatly in the bottom ivory envelope.

She knew she shouldn't read the letters. That would be very rude and beneath her. She was not a snoop.

Charlotte would be back any minute. How horrible for her to return and find Addie reading through her personal letters from her future groom!

But Charlotte's story and Addie's curiosity won over her better judgement. Addie would just take a little peek. Just to see if Charlotte mentioned how God had spoken to her. Yes, that was what Addie was looking for. Charlotte had said that she really wanted to answer her questions. But that would be impossible now. Charlotte was taking far too long tending to her personal needs.

One letter. That was all. Once Addie made up her mind, she slowly unfolded the paper with her gloved fingers, placing the other envelopes securely in her lap, along with the ticket.

A picture fell out. At the sight of the man's face staring back at her, Addie forgot about the letter. She let the paper drop softly to her lap and held the portrait with both hands. It wasn't a typical portrait. Instead of a suit, Joshua had posed in his ranch clothes and hat that concealed all but a little dark hair peeking from beneath. He looked proud and had a strong, masculine jaw that hinted of stubbornness. Joshua Harding looked every inch a rugged man of the West.

But Addie liked his eyes most. They were honest and kind. Her own fiancé's eyes were cold and devoid of emotion, especially when they looked at her.

With her gloved finger, she gently touched Joshua Harding's face, feeling an intense longing that Charlotte's fiancé was the one meeting her at the end of the line, not her own.

A long train whistle followed by two short ones jarred Addie from the picture.

She looked around frantically. Where was Charlotte?

The train was going to leave without her! She gently laid the picture back in the carpet bag with the others and popped back up off the bench, desperately searching the platform for a hint of Charlotte's blonde hair.

The crowds were larger now as people rushed to their trains. What was she going to do? She didn't have her tickets to Denver. They were tucked into her own carpet bag, the one currently in Charlotte's possession.

Addie pushed her way through the passersby, positioning herself directly in front of the steps to the train. She dug out Charlotte's ticket and gripped it tightly in her hand. When Charlotte came, she would quickly trade her bags and the ticket so the other woman could board quickly.

Charlotte had been gone so long that Addie was now in danger of missing her own train. What if her train left before she found Charlotte? Papa would be so angry.

For a moment the train station melted away, replaced in her mind by another depot. She imagined her train arriving in Denver without her. Addie was a bride-to-be as well. But there was a difference. Charlotte chose to be a bride. Addie was being forced into an arranged marriage with the son of one of her father's business partners.

Well, not partner yet. Addie was being offered as a token gift to seal the profitable partnership between a railroad baron and her father, the merchant. Her father stood to make a great deal of money if Isaac Trenton saw her fit to be a bride for his son, Blake.

Addie was being sent to Denver to be inspected and to determine if she would be suitable. A lot was at stake in this 'business transaction' as Addie's father had told her before sending her out the door and on her way alone to Denver.

She was not to fail her father now. It was her responsibility as the only child of Moses Delaney to follow through. After all, she had already failed him by being born a girl.

Addie's thoughts shifted once again to her arrival in Denver. Blake might be there to meet her, but most likely not. She had met him once before in New York when he came with his father to discuss terms with Moses. Blake had made it clear then that he didn't want this marriage any more than she did. He would most likely send a servant, if anyone at all to meet her at the station. Addie's arrival would not bring nearly the excitement and anticipation that Charlotte's would in Texas.

The conductor's voice thrust Addie from her painful thoughts.

"Miss, is this your train? Will you be traveling to Texas today? The train is ready to leave."

"No, please wait a few more minutes." Addie paused, searching for a way to describe her association with Charlotte. She racked her mind, but found herself reluctantly saying, "I have my friend's ticket. She should be here any moment."

"We can't wait, Miss." The conductor glanced at his pocket watch. "We have a schedule to keep."

Charlotte was going to miss her train. There would be no mail order bride arriving in Last Chance to meet Joshua Harding. At that moment, Charlotte's words came back to Addie, as if whispered on a welcome breeze. "Everything happens for a reason. We might not understand God's plan, but He is still in control. You have to go where God leads you, and He will take care of the rest." Could this be God's will for Addie?

In one gloved hand, Addie held a ticket to a new life, a chance to get away from her arranged marriage. In her other hand, she carried Charlotte's carpet bag, packed with handwritten letters by a man with kind eyes—a man who wanted a bride, a companion to spend his life with. Not someone who was bound by an arranged marriage. Blake Trenton didn't want a bride. Joshua Harding did.

"Last call, Miss. The train is leaving with or without your friend."

Addie searched the crowds one last time for Charlotte. Seeing no trace of her bench companion, Addie raised her chin a fraction and turned to the train, her mind made up.

"Here's my ticket, sir. I will be going to Texas today."

Chapter 2

Last Chance, Texas

WITH a deep breath, Addie rose from her seat and walked down the narrow aisle of the train. Every other passenger had disembarked ahead of her, and she now had no excuse to delay. In a few days, she very well could be walking down a different aisle, this time in a church. Was she really going to go through with this? What was she thinking! She couldn't pose as Charlotte Mason from Atlanta, Georgia! She was Adelaide Delaney from New York City. Furthermore, could she really deceive Joshua?

Throughout her journey, Addie had read all the letters bound by the blue ribbon. She knew it was wrong, but she couldn't seem to stop herself. The man in the picture drew her like no man had ever before. Something in his eyes made Addie lose all reason.

Even now, despite her better judgment, her body moved forward, then down the steps of the train to the platform.

Before Addie could fully take in her surroundings, her gaze collided with eyes that had haunted her sleep and driven her to recklessly alter her life's course. He was here. Waiting for her. Well, Addie amended, waiting for Charlotte.

A slow smile spread across Joshua's face as he stepped forward from where he leaned at the corner of the building.

Addie found herself smiling in return, her heart beating frantically. He was every bit as handsome, if not more so, than his picture. Dark brown hair, almost black, and piercing eyes that, even from a distance, seemed to burn with an icy fire.

Addie's breath came out in short gasps.

As if drawn by an unseen force, she moved to meet him, stepping off the platform, her boots touching the red Texas soil for the first time.

Instead of a black and white version of Joshua, the full-color, living, breathing version stood right in front of her. And his eyes were blue.

He was only a few short steps away. His hand reached for her.

She suddenly had an overwhelming urge to feel the touch of his hand. As ridiculous as it seemed, Addie felt that with that single, initial touch, Joshua would either recognize her as an impostor or as the woman he was meant to be with.

But the question was to remain unanswered.

For at that moment, when she slowly reached her hand to

his, they missed. Addie's right foot slipped out from under her. Her arms flailed as she struggled for balance, sending Charlotte's infamous carpet bag flying out of her grasp to, once again, rain undergarments onto the dusty street.

"Whoa, I've got you." Strong arms caught her gently, halting her descent mere inches from the ground. "Are you alright?"

Addie clutched the soft cotton of Joshua's shirt.

"I'm so sorry," Addie stammered, embarrassed by her display of uncharacteristic bad grace. "I must have slipped in some mud."

"I'm afraid that's not mud."

Joshua righted Addie to her feet, and she had her first opportunity to see and smell what lay beneath her boots. Manure. Heat flooded Addie's face as she stepped back to the safety of the platform and took in the damage to her boots as well as the hem of her dress.

She still wore her expensive navy traveling suit, with its long tailored jacket atop her bustled skirt. She hadn't been able to overcome her aversion to Charlotte's ugly brown dress from the bag, refusing to trade it for her own stylish traveling suit, so she had kept her own. After all, she wanted to look her best when meeting Joshua.

Now she wished she had not been so temperamental. Better to ruin Charlotte's dress than her own!

"Are you by chance Charlotte Mason?" Joshua asked, stepping up to join Addie on the platform.

Here was the moment Addie had agonized over as her train had covered the miles to its destination. She looked up to the man who towered above her, meeting blue eyes that searched her own. They were so honest and kind. She couldn't lie to this man. She was a Christian.

Addie opened her mouth, ready to tell her story and reveal that she wasn't his bride, when he bent to pick up something from the street.

"Well, I think this answers my question."

Addie's breath caught. He held the letters with the cornflower ribbon. She started to shake her head.

But Joshua had begun to smile again, causing her to literally forget her real name.

"Do you have a trunk?" Joshua asked, seemingly oblivious to his effect on her.

"I believe so," Addie said, turning and looking down the length of the long train, wondering where they would unload the passengers' luggage. She sincerely hoped Charlotte's trunk boasted a large label. Otherwise, she had no hope of identifying it!

The platform stretched behind her, the board walkway extending a good distance down the track. Addie saw workers loading and unloading crates way down the line, but other than those, there were very few people loitering nearby.

Last Chance was not a major train station. While they had a restaurant and sleeping facilities for train passengers, the building behind the platform looked inconsequential, especially compared to the vast rangeland surrounding it. As the train had pulled up to the town, Addie had thought the cluster of buildings dubbed Last Chance, Texas, looked like a handful of trash scattered around the train tracks. It was not an impressive town. Addie figured the only features that had even earned Last Chance a train stop was the necessity of water and the proximity of large cattle ranches.

Even now, the engineer and rail workers prepared the train to move forward on the loop through Texas cattle country. There was little need to stay long when there were other stops to make before the track circled back to a larger junction.

Addie turned back from her perusal of the town to find Joshua looking at her with a rather silly half grin.

"What is it?" she asked, self-consciously reaching up to brush her nose lightly with her glove. She prayed none of the dirt or manure had managed to make it up that far.

Joshua ducked his head in an adorable, almost bashful manner, as if he'd been caught and felt reluctant to give a confession. Finally, he looked back up to return her gaze directly. "I'm sorry," he apologized. "You're just not at all what I expected."

Instant alarm shot through Addie. One of her many panicking episodes on the train had been when struck by the thought that Charlotte might have sent Joshua a picture, in which case, he would immediately know Addie was not his bride. Addie had tried to tell herself that Charlotte had likely never been able to afford a portrait, but she worried nonetheless. Now it seemed that concern had become reality.

In her shame, Addie struggled to keep eye contact as Joshua spoke.

"I know from your letters that you are a good Christian woman and have a loving, wonderful heart. I tried to tell myself that was enough. However, since I never saw a picture of you, I was a little concerned that you might have two heads or thirteen toes. I told myself it didn't matter. I know that true beauty is found in the soul of a person, but I'm not a complete saint. I am a man who thoroughly appreciates that a beautiful woman has come to be his bride."

Addie laughed nervously. He thought she was beautiful! Well, on the outside at least. Manure on her feet and all! "Well, you can see I don't have two heads, but I can't promise about the thirteen toes."

Though Joshua's words had thrilled her, they'd also concerned her. What if Joshua was already in love with Charlotte Mason? Would her looks be enough? Could Addie even compete with the good, spiritual Charlotte? To cover her sudden insecurity, Addie once again bent to fill the carpet bag.

Joshua followed suit, thankfully choosing the least personal garments to pack.

"There you are, Josh!" An older man, with a round belly and gray hair thinning on top hurried across the train platform as fast as his short legs could carry him.

Addie jerked her head up and dropped the night cap she had been folding into the bag. At the sight of this person coming toward them, Addie had an awful premonition.

The little man in front of her wore the customary black suit with a white stripe peeking out from under his double chin.

Addie gulped and struggled to rise, her legs tangled in her skirts.

"Hello, Reverend Gates." Joshua replied, straightening from where he had been picking up the wayward clothes.

Joshua quickly offered her his hand.

"Thank you." Addie muttered quietly, her eyes never leaving the man in black.

"Reverend, may I introduce you to Miss Charlotte Mason, my bride."

Addie felt a small thrill at the pride in Joshua's voice.

"It's a pleasure to meet you, Miss Mason. I'm Reverend Arthur Gates, the circuit preacher for around these parts. I feel I have you at a disadvantage, Miss Mason. I already know you, but you don't know me!"

Terror sliced through Addie. What did he mean? Had he met Charlotte previously? If so, then he would soon know that Addie was an impostor!

Lifting her gaze to bravely meet the reverend, she saw that his sweat-shined face beamed only mild curiosity.

"Josh consulted me prior to placing his advertisement in the newspaper," he explained. "He wanted my opinion about searching for a wife. I hope you don't mind, but Josh has been sharing with me brief snatches of your letters. I was pleased when I read your testimony because then I knew for certain: the Lord has answered our prayers and blessed Josh with a godly bride!"

Testimony? Oh, no! What had Charlotte said? Addie knew very little of Charlotte's life. She had read Joshua's letters to Charlotte, but she didn't have the other piece of the puzzle—Charlotte's letters to him. That lack of information could be Addie's undoing!

Unknowingly leaving Addie with her thoughts in a swirling mess, the reverend turned his attention to Joshua.

"I'm so glad that I found you before the train leaves," Reverend Gates said, taking out a snowy white handkerchief from the traveling case he held. He began mopping his sweating brow.

"Are you headed somewhere, Reverend?" Joshua asked, surprise lacing his voice.

"Indeed I am, young man," he replied, bobbing his head vigorously. "I know you had planned to wait a few days before having me officiate at your wedding, but unfortunately, I just received a telegram this morning that I am needed in Perdition. An urgent matter has arisen."

"Is it something serious?"

"Well, no, not exactly. It seems there was a rather unfortunate incident regarding last Sunday's church potluck. Harold Duncan got sick shortly afterward, and a disagreement ensued as to whether Priscilla Marrow's fried chicken or Mary Winter's deviled eggs are to blame. The congregation is quite at odds over it and threatening to hold separate services tomorrow. I must hurry to help calm the waters, so to speak. Which brings us to my reason for searching you out. After I have smoothed the ruffled feathers in Perdition, I will continue on with my usual loop. It will be a month before I am back here in Last Chance. If you want me to perform the ceremony before I leave, we need to do so now. I have only a few minutes before my train departs."

Addie's breath caught. "Today?" she squeaked. Addie immediately began to tremble. What had she done? She thought she would have more time before the actual wedding. She thought she could talk to Joshua, explain who she really was.

She had to stop this!

Turning to Joshua, she took a deep breath and began,

"Mr. Harding, I'm not—"

A train whistle muffled her words. What was it with train whistles interrupting important conversations!

"Reverend, would you mind giving Charlotte and me a few minutes?"

"Certainly!" the man replied, immediately turning to wander across the platform and speak with a grizzled man leaning against a post outside the depot.

Joshua turned toward her, taking her hands into his own. His hands were large and sun-bronzed, with rough calluses on his palms. "Charlotte, I know this is rushed. But I'm ready to marry you. Will you marry me today?"

Addie gazed into Joshua's icy blue eyes, her mouth moving and forming words her brain hadn't had the time to fully process. "Yes."

Wait, what? Did she actually say, yes?

"I mean, no. Well, I mean no, not now. Not no, never."

Addie took a deep breath and tried again. "I mean, yes, I will marry you, I just need a little time."

So much for the conviction that Adelaide Delaney didn't stutter!

Addie glanced nervously at Reverend Gates, forcing herself to slow her breathing. "Are you sure he can't come back in a few days? Just so we will have time to get to know each other a little more?" Addie turned back to Joshua, her eyes pleading for understanding.

"I know that this is sudden," Joshua squeezed her shaking hands slightly. "I had planned to wait a few days before getting married. But I can't put you up in the hotel for a month, and it wouldn't be proper for you to stay at the ranch with me unless we are married. I know we just met, but I don't want to wait to marry you."

Joshua paused, waiting until she looked him squarely. With all sincerity, he finally continued. "Even if we marry today, I will wait for a full marriage until you are ready. I can feel your hands shaking. I know you're frightened that it's all happening so fast. But don't be scared of me, Charlotte. I will never hurt you or force you to do anything you do not want to do. This marriage will be in name only, until you are ready to make it otherwise."

Addie breathed a sigh of relief. She could do this. They wouldn't consummate the marriage, so it technically wasn't a real marriage. If things weren't going well, she could just back out, right?

Not trusting herself to speak, Addie took in a shuddering breath, and nodded.

Chapter 3

"WE'RE ready, Reverend." Joshua called across the platform.

"Wonderful!" Reverend Gates returned, clapping his hands together in approval. "I was just speaking to George here, and he has agreed to serve as a witness to your marriage."

"Thank you, George." Joshua shook hands with the same dusty cowboy who had been leaning against the post.

Addie had to fight hard not to reach for her handkerchief to cover her nose. George stank! Was it a bad omen that their only wedding attendant was a smelly cowboy dressed in a sweat-stained shirt, a dented cowboy hat on his head, with pants that had probably never seen a decent scrubbing? Addie highly doubted that he had taken a bath in months, if ever.

"I'm plumb tickled to do it, Josh! Mighty nice to be a witness for once, instead of being witnessed at!" George wheezed out a laugh at his own joke, then turned to Addie. "Well, ain't she a looker! I'll have to send me away for one of them mail order brides. Do they all look like her? Wowee!"

"Oh, George, why would you send away for a woman when you've got me?" A woman sashayed up to George, looping her arm through his, and smiling at Addie. She wore a shockingly low-cut dress, in an equally startling shade of crimson. "Do you need another witness, Reverend? I'm happy to be of service."

"Um, yes, of course, Miss Faye." The reverend, looking rather uneasy, continued, "That is, if it meets with your approval, Josh."

"Of course. Thank you, ma'am," Josh said, dipping his head politely. "That is most kind of you."

"No trouble at all," the woman crooned. "I just happened to be in the area checking to see if maybe some train passengers were in search of *accommodations*. I'm not needed at The Painted Lady for a few minutes still."

Painted Lady? This woman was a saloon girl! Now she had a smelly cowboy and a saloon girl as the only guests to her train depot wedding! This trip was not turning out at all how she had expected.

"Just let me get my Bible." Reverend Gates hastened to open his traveling case, retrieving a well-worn Bible with fraying edges. "Here it is. Now let's begin."

The next few moments were a blur as Addie tried to focus on the words that the preacher spoke. She was getting married! To a man she didn't know. With manure on her skirt and boots! What would her father think when he found out? Thankfully, New York was a very long way from Texas, and she felt grateful for that distance. For the first time in her life, Addie was breaking free of the expectations thrust upon her by having the last name Delaney.

This realization brought a smile to her face, which didn't fade until Reverend Gates turned to her and said, "Do you, Charlotte Mason, take this man to be your husband?"

Addie had forgotten about the wedding vows. This really would be a farce of a marriage, because she was not Charlotte Mason!

Joshua looked at her expectantly, and Addie rushed to fill the sudden silence. "Oh, yes. I mean, I do."

Joshua said his vows, and slid a simple gold band that he had produced from his shirt pocket, onto Addie's left ring finger.

"I now pronounce you husband and wife. You may kiss your bride."

Joshua leaned forward slowly. Addie's eyes slid shut as she felt the whisper-soft touch of Joshua's lips on her own. Before she was even certain it had happened, it was over and the reverend was vigorously pumping Joshua's hand in congratulations.

With a quick "God bless you," the reverend hurried off to board the waiting train, leaving as swiftly as he arrived.

The grizzled cowboy and the saloon girl waved their goodbyes, drifting down the street, their laughter fading as they disappeared into a clapboard building.

Addie stood alone on the platform with her new husband. Or was he really Charlotte's husband? Addie wasn't quite sure.

One thing was for certain, though. Addie had gotten herself into a huge mess.

"Are you ready to go see your new home, Charlotte?" Joshua smiled.

Addie demurely nodded, though she couldn't quite stop the answering smile that lifted the corners of her mouth at the thought of a new home with Joshua Harding.

"Let me locate your trunk," Joshua said, looking down the long line of the now empty railroad tracks. "Oh, it must be this one over here. It's the only one left."

Sure enough, one lonely traveling trunk stood at the other end of the platform, it's wood sides scarred and dented from many years of use. Addie followed in Joshua's wake, breathing a sigh of relief when she saw "Mason" stamped on a brass placard under the front clasp. Was it too much to hope that Charlotte would have something in this truck that was nicer to wear than the brown dress in the carpet bag?

Joshua lifted the trunk easily onto his shoulder, and proceeded toward a rustic-looking buckboard wagon. Addie's footsteps slowed. Joshua was a cattle rancher. Surely he had a nicer wagon than this? It wasn't the worst wagon Addie had ever seen, but it wasn't the fine carriages she was used to.

Joshua set Charlotte's trunk into the back with a thud. "I'll go get your carpet bag as well." Addie almost said to leave it. That broken bag had caused her so much humiliation! But it was also the bag that brought her to Texas, so she refrained.

Joshua returned quickly with Addie's nemesis, stowing

it next to the trunk.

"Thank you, Mr. Harding," Addie said, accepting the hand he offered as he helped her climb onto the seat of the wagon.

"I think we can drop the formalities a little, Charlotte. After all, we are married now. You can call me Josh."

"Not Joshua?"

"I think my mother was the only person who ever called me by my full name. And that was only when I was a few seconds away from her taking a switch to my hide for getting into some type of tomfoolery. If you called me Joshua, I might take off running, thinking you had a stick in your hand!"

"Oh, I see," Addie replied, returning Josh's smile. Since they were discussing name preferences, perhaps now would be a good time to tell him to call her Addie. Her actions seemed a little less sinful if he used her own name, and not the name of the woman whose fiancé she had stolen. It was a first step toward the truth.

"Josh," Addie began nervously, "would you mind terribly if you called me Addie instead of Charlotte?"

"Addie?" Josh repeated, looking doubtful. "Why Addie?"

"Well, no one calls me Charlotte." That part was truthful as well. She was making great strides with her honesty.

Josh looked quizzically at Addie as he took the reigns and gave a quick tap on the back of the buckskin horse that was hitched to the wagon.

"I've never heard of Addie being a nickname for Charlotte. Lottie, yes. Even Charlie, maybe. But Addie?"

Josh shook his dark head.

"It's a childhood nickname," Addie rushed to explain, still trying to maintain as much of the truth as possible, but hoping to halt the suspicious glances he kept throwing her way. "My family called me Addie, well, because I was... I was... I was addled a lot?"

Good grief, Addie! Why did you say that? He's going to think you are crazy!

Not to mention she had just lied!

"No, I mean they teased me that I was addled. But I wasn't really. I can think clearly. Really. Oh, for pity sake! Just call me Charlotte!"

Josh began to laugh. "Actually, I think Addie is perfect. It seems to suit you."

Addie's sharp retort died as it met the gleam of Josh's teasing blue eyes.

She slowly exhaled, trying to calm her nerves so she wouldn't say something else to make him think she was *addled*!

It would be her own fault if he thought her mentally befuddled. What had happened to the cool, refined Adelaide Delaney from New York City? Ever since she had stepped off the train into Last Chance, Texas, she had been nothing but addle-brained. And there was one person to blame for her inability to think clearly, and he sat beside her now, grinning from ear to ear.

Trying to gain back some of her dignity, Addie set her shoulders and lifted her chin before changing the subject off of her supposed "nickname."

"You mentioned that your mother called you by your full

name," she said quietly. "I was sorry to read in your letters of her recent passing."

The minute the words left her lips, she wished she could grab them back.

The grin and warm, teasing lights in Josh's eyes were immediately snuffed out by the shadow cast by her words.

She had been so determined to switch the subject off her, that she hadn't considered the topic or how it may affect Josh. Just more proof that she really was addled!

"Thank you," Josh said softly, his gaze turning from her to study the road in front of them. "I guess you and I have a lot in common where family is concerned. Neither of us have any siblings, and both of us are orphans now."

Addie shifted uncomfortably. He had a lot in common with Charlotte. Addie's father was still very much alive. Was he even at this moment searching for her? Had he received word that she hadn't made it to Denver?

"How did you get into the cattle business?" Addie asked, hoping to find a safer topic. Josh's few letters to Charlotte had been very factual, but had little information on him or his background. Addie knew exactly how many cattle were in Josh's last cattle drive, but she couldn't really know if he had friends or even if he liked "cow farming."

"Was your father a rancher?" Addie continued, barely remembering the correct term for his profession.

"Yes, he and my uncle started the Bar H. When my father died, his half became mine. My uncle lives at the ranch as well. You will meet him tomorrow. The sun is starting to set, so by the time we get home, he will have already bunked down for the night."

"Do you think your uncle will be upset that he missed the wedding?" Addie asked, suddenly worried that she wouldn't make a good impression.

"No, Pete isn't like that," Josh assured, grinning like he couldn't help but find the idea rather comical. "Pete usually tries to avoid weddings. And women in general. He wasn't happy about my intentions to search for a bride."

"Why?"

"He thinks women are bad luck on a ranch."

Addie's face fell. That didn't sound promising. Josh's only living family member disliked her already, sight unseen.

"But don't worry," Josh comforted, seeming to notice her distress. "You said in your letters that you love to cook. Uncle Pete might not like women much, but he loves food. You'll win him over."

Addie was in serious trouble.

Having grown up in a wealthy household with a fleet of servants at her beck and call, she hadn't needed to be domestic.

"I thought you said in your letters that you had a cook? Was I mistaken? Not that I wouldn't help out, of course." Although how much help she actually was, remained to be seen, having never lifted a spoon to cook anything in her life. But cooking couldn't be that difficult. She was fluent in Latin, she played the piano and sang, and she could embroider beautifully. She could learn to cook.

Josh's brow furrowed. "Hank? He's the cook for the ranch hands. I wouldn't call what he stirs up food."

"Then why do you employ him if he is so terrible?"

"Hank has been with my family for years. The Bar H is his home. I would never run him out of a job." Josh smiled. "But I am looking forward to good home-cooked meals for a change. That's for sure."

"Is that why you wanted a bride?" Addie asked uncertainly. "Because you wanted a cook?"

"Oh, definitely."

Addie could tell by Josh's smirk that he was teasing her, but doubts plagued her. They continued for a few minutes in silence as the wagon rumbled down the bumpy dirt path that cut through the landscape. Grass grew plentiful here, baked golden in the Texas heat. Addie had never seen such wide open spaces.

"Are those your cattle over there?" She asked, tilting her head to indicate a herd not far from them.

"Yes, see the white H with a straight bar on the left flank of that steer?"

Addie had no idea where to look for a 'flank,' but she refused to ask Josh and reveal how little she knew of farm life.

"That's the Bar H's brand," Josh explained. "All of our cattle are marked with that symbol to distinguish our cattle from others."

Addie gestured with her gloved hand. "So this is your land we are on now?"

"Yes. We own this land and the water rights to the creek that flows nearby."

"How big is your ranch?" Addie really didn't intend to interrogate him, but she'd just married the man. Suddenly every detail about him seemed vitally important.

"The Bar H is the largest ranch in the area," Josh explained patiently, not seeming to mind Addie's inquisition. "We own over 100,000 acres."

"That seems like a lot of land," Addie said carefully, hoping her lack of knowledge wasn't off-putting to Josh. "How do you keep track of all of your cattle?"

"We have a dozen or more ranch hands to help out. More so during cattle drives. Until recently, most of the cattle in Texas was free range. But that is starting to change with the rise of cattle rustlers. We are now working on fencing in our property."

They were quiet again for a few moments, each lost in their own thoughts as the sun started to dip below the horizon.

"We are getting close to the ranch house now," Josh said, indicating the direction with a nod of his head. "Just over that rise, and you should see it."

Addie leaned forward, straining to catch her first glimpse of her new home. Sure enough, within minutes, buildings began to take shape.

"That's the bunkhouse over on the left. Uncle Pete's cabin is next to it, and the main house is the structure by that copse of trees."

Addie took little note of the other buildings and corrals Josh indicated. Her eyes were fixed solely on the house. Darkness had begun to fall, so she couldn't see it as well as she would have liked, but at the sight of those shadowy structures, she felt peace and warmth steal over her.

Her home.

It wasn't as elaborate as her father's house in New York,

but she loved it already. It was painted white, with a long, narrow one story base, and a two story attachment.

"When my father and uncle first settled here, the single story was the main house," Josh explained. "Later, after my father married my mother, he added the two story wing."

Josh set the brake, and climbed down from the seat. "Let me help you inside. I will give you a tour, and then we can see if Hank has left us some dinner. I'm sure you're hungry. We've had quite the afternoon."

"Howdy, boss!" A man's voice yelled as Josh helped Addie from the wagon. Two men approached from the direction of the bunkhouse.

"Hello, Clint. Wyatt. This here is Addie Harding, my wife."

He had called her Addie! And his wife! Addie fairly glowed with joy from her new title.

"Pleased to meet you, ma'am," the taller of the two said, quickly removing his hat.

"It's lovely to meet you as well," Addie responded.

"Can you boys grab Addie's trunk and bag from the wagon, and then unhitch Roan? I will show Addie around the house." Josh guided her to the front door, his warm hand on the small of her back.

After opening the door, Josh turned and swept Addie into his arms.

Her breath caught. She instinctively put her arms around his neck as her eyes flew to his.

Holding her gaze steady, he slowly stepped through the doorway, carrying her over the threshold. "Welcome home,

Mrs. Harding."

His soft, deep voice sent thrills down her spine and sent her heart to fluttering like a trapped butterfly.

Much too soon, her boots touched the floor. He set her down gently, though the instant he let her go, she felt bereft, longing again for the warmth of his touch.

Josh took her room-by-room showing her the kitchen, parlor, and his office.

Midway through the tour, the tall cowboy Addie met earlier arrived with her trunk.

"Thank you, Clint," Josh said. "Go ahead and take it upstairs."

The man did as directed, and disappeared up the stairs, only to return moments later, tipping his hat in Addie's direction as he left.

"I think that covers the rooms down here." Climbing the stairs, Josh pointed to doors on the left of the hallway, "those are the guest rooms, and this one on the right is ours."

Addie paused in the doorway, thinking she had heard Josh incorrectly. Josh had said this marriage was in name only. Surely she would be staying in one of the guest rooms.

With Josh waiting for her to enter, she stepped cautiously into the large room. Before she could take an initial survey, her eyes focused on one item, and she stopped in her tracks. Startled at her sudden halt, Josh bumped into her from behind, yet Addie was frozen, standing like a piece of furniture.

A pair of white drawers lay sprawled on the floor, likely forgotten by the then bachelor, Josh, that morning. Right next to Josh's underwear, nestled close to the bed stood

Charlotte's trunk.

Only it was Charlotte's no more. It was now Addie's trunk, and it was sitting in a room that belonged to a man.

And Addie was his wife.

Chapter 4

"ADDIE, what's wrong?" Josh asked, concern lacing his voice.

Addie tried to get the words out, but they wouldn't move through her constricting throat.

It had been an agonizing hour since she'd first seen her trunk in Josh's room. She'd tried to act normal and brush it off. But the image of her trunk right by Josh's white drawers had haunted her. She hadn't been able to eat two bites of dinner or hold any semblance of a conversation with Josh. He had shot her curious glances, but she had still been unable to muster up the courage needed to tell him what was wrong.

Trudging back up the stairs after dinner, she felt like she might be sick. Josh's footsteps had clomped up the steps behind her, and her heart beat about triple time to the rhythm.

At the top of the stairs, the candle Josh carried cast dancing shadows on the walls. They seemed eerie and almost alive, only accentuating Addie's fear.

With heavy feet mechanically trudging forward, she had finally made it to the bedroom. Just like before, she stopped at the sight of the trunk, unable to move forward.

She closed her eyes and tried to breathe deeply, yet it didn't make a difference. She couldn't do this!

Then Josh's question had reached through her fog of fear, gently questioning what was wrong.

Finally finding her voice, Addie murmured, "I'd like to stay in the guest room, please."

Josh took Addie's shoulders and turned her to face him. Lifting her chin with one finger, so that she was forced to look into his eyes, he said, "As I told you before, you have nothing to fear from me."

"Then why must I stay in this room?" she asked, her voice small.

"This is our room. I don't want to start a precedent of sleeping in separate rooms. If we quarrel, which I'm sure we will from time-to-time, I don't want it to be normal for us to be apart. I meant what I said at the depot. I am a man of my word. You are safe with me."

Addie let out the breath she didn't realize she held.

Placing a gentle kiss on Addie's forehead, Josh said, "I still have to go check on the horses. Clementine's foal is due any day now. Why don't you get ready for bed in peace while your big, scary husband is busy."

Addie managed to meet Josh's eyes with a shaky smile

before he handed her a candle and disappeared.

Addie set the candle on the tall bureau that lined a wall in the bedroom. An oil lamp waited beside the candle, but Addie didn't bother to light it. She realized she might not have much time before Josh returned. If she hurried, she might even be asleep! Or at the very least she could pretend to be.

Not even attempting to survey the room in the flickering candlelight, Addie immediately flew into action, unbuttoning her traveling dress, stripping off her undergarments and her soiled boots. She rushed about the room, unwinding her hair from her bun, pouring water from a white pitcher into a basin atop a small bureau, then splashing it on her face.

However, the water felt so good, she couldn't resist taking a cloth and quickly cleaning the rest of herself, all the while shooting nervous glances at the door. Unfortunately, there would be no real bath tonight at this late hour, but after so many days on the train, Addie felt sore and grimy. She would repair what damage she could with a cloth and a little soap, but she promised herself a real bath before the sun rose high tomorrow morning. She had definitely earned a good long soak after traveling across the country.

While she had found lodging along the way at several stations, which had allowed her to clean and rest, this last leg of the journey from St. Louis had been the most difficult. Though she had been able to purchase food with the money she kept in the hidden pocket of her dress, Charlotte's ticket didn't come with the comfortable seats of the more costly train cars. Also, since Charlotte's bag hadn't been as well-stocked as Addie's, the tin of crackers hadn't lasted long in between stops. Somehow her makeshift toilette tonight didn't quite rid herself of the discomfort from the past few days.

Promising herself a real bath tomorrow, she rushed to the trunk to find something to wear. Not bothering to peruse the trunk's contents, she simply grabbed the first nightgown she could find and hoped it would be plenty ugly. She knew Josh had promised not to touch her, but in her mind, the uglier the nightgown, the better chance Josh had of keeping his good intentions. Quickly, she tugged the sack-like gown over her head; gave one brush to her long, blonde hair, and she was done.

Yanking back the blankets, Addie hastily climbed into bed.

Drat! She forgot to blow out the candle! Forget it. She was already in bed, and didn't want to risk Josh walking in while she extinguished the flame. Burying herself deeper under the colorful quilts, she pulled the sheet over her face as high as it would reach.

And then she waited.

Every squeak of the floorboards sent her heart racing, convinced that Josh was on his way up the stairs. But he never came.

Where was he? Perhaps he was delayed? Was Clementine's foal coming? Or maybe Josh had decided to sleep in the bunkhouse. Or downstairs in the parlor. Or his office.

But why would he do that? He was the one who had said he didn't want to 'start a precedent.'

But why did she care? She should be happy that she was alone. She had the bed to herself, and she could stretch out as far as she wanted and not worry about touching him.

What a splendid idea. That's exactly what she would do. She stretched her arms and legs as far as she could, relaxing her aching muscles. Yes, this was definitely for the best. Her eyelids grew heavy.

Images floated through her mind. Josh's face. The train. Charlotte.

Drifting somewhere between sleep and awake, Addie imagined Charlotte in her ugly brown dress standing face-to-face with her. Then, as she watched, Charlotte's brown dress transformed into Addie's traveling suit.

Something brushed Addie's leg.

Addie let out a startled yelp. Something was under the covers!

Quilts tangled around her waist as she rolled off the bed, landing in a heap of linens with her legs sticking out like the drumsticks on a chicken.

A voice called from the top of the bed. "If you are done rolling around on the floor down there, I would like to get some sleep. Oh, and can I have my blanket back? I didn't know I married such a bed hog."

"You!" Addie sputtered as Josh poked his head over the side of the bed.

"Who exactly were you expecting? Should I be concerned?"

"I didn't hear you come in!" Addie accused. "You startled me!"

"I'm not surprised with the way you were snoring and all."

"I don't snore!" Addie insisted.

"Could have fooled me. Maybe I should sleep out in the bunkhouse with the ranch hands. It may be quieter."

Addie could tell by the sparkle in his eyes and the way his mouth kept fighting off a grin that Josh was teasing her.

"Here, let me help you up," Josh said, extending his hand toward her.

"No, thank you. I am quite comfortable down here." Addie crossed her arms, and raised her chin in defiance. She did not enjoy being the brunt of his joking, and she certainly didn't want to join him in bed!

"Oh, I'm sure you are," Josh agreed. "The mice will keep you good company."

Addie launched herself off the floor in one mighty leap. Unfortunately, she had not planned her destination. Instead of plopping softly on the bed, she landed squarely on a startled Josh's back.

"Mice!" Addie shrieked. "I hate mice! Are there really mice in here? Answer me, Joshua Harding!"

"I would, but I can't breathe." Josh said, his voice muffled, his face pressed into the mattress.

"Oh." Addie quickly relocated to the top of the bed, searching for a blanket to cover herself with.

Unfortunately, there were none. They were all on the floor. With the mice.

Addie shuddered.

"There, that's better." Josh rolled to his side, gazing at her huddled against the oak head board. "There are no mice in the house. I just said that to get you off of the floor."

"Are you sure?"

"Yes, we have several cats who keep the mice population in check."

Josh leaned over, dragging pillows and bedding back onto it.

Seeing Josh in his long johns brought an immediate blush to her face, but she refused to give in to the embarrassment. Instead, she grabbed a pillow and threw it at him, hitting his grinning head squarely on target. "Don't ever scare me like that again!"

Josh laughed, tossing the harmless pillow back on the bed. "Scare you with mice, or climbing into bed?"

"Both!"

"Duly noted," Josh said with a rakish grin.

Addie huffed indignantly, turning on her side, away from where Josh settled back in bed.

Josh blew out the candle. The room instantly shrouded in darkness. Though she was wide awake, all of Addie's nervousness had melted away. She listened as Josh's breathing slowly lengthened and evened out. When she was convinced he was asleep, she finally allowed her own breathing to match his. Then she drifted to sleep with the gentle rumble of Josh's soft laughter echoing through her memory.

 *Chapter 5*

"THERE, that wasn't so difficult," Addie said, wiping her hands on the white apron she had tied around her waist. The bacon lay in the pan, the stove was lit, and Josh was going to be so impressed when she served him a delicious breakfast her first morning at the ranch. He would never know that she hadn't cooked a day in her life.

Earlier that morning, Addie had awoken to an empty bed. Judging by the coolness of the sheets, Josh had long since left to start the morning chores.

Addie had taken her time selecting the prettiest dress she could find in Charlotte's trunk, an emerald green gingham with gold buttons on the bodice. Clearly, it had been Charlotte's 'Sunday best.' It was the only suitable dress in the entire trunk. All the others, and there were only two, were varying shades of dull gray and brown.

She would have to talk to Josh later about locating a seamstress in town to make her a proper wardrobe. On the bright side, at least she and Charlotte were close to the same size. The dress hugged Addie's trim waist perfectly before flaring out gently to the floor. Straining to see herself in the small oval mirror above the bureau, she had to admit that although the dress was not nearly as sophisticated as she was used to, it flattered her figure and even seemed to bring out flecks of green in her sapphire eyes.

The mirror was another matter Addie intended to discuss with Josh. He must use the bedroom mirror only for shaving, because it was entirely too small to serve any other purpose. Addie intended to purchase a larger mirror as soon as possible. She felt confident Josh wouldn't protest her new wardrobe, or a larger mirror, especially if she asked him while he was eating a delicious home-cooked meal.

With her goals firmly in mind, Addie had set out to cook Josh a breakfast to properly earn her the title, 'rancher's wife.'

However, second thoughts pounced almost immediately after entering the kitchen. The large cast-iron stove dominated one corner of the kitchen, looming large and intimidating. She supposed it was a nice, newer piece of equipment, as far as stoves were concerned, but she had no idea where to start.

The stove had been slightly warm to the touch, and a kettle of coffee rested on its dark surface. After opening and closing the doors and turning knobs on the side, she had located the firebox at the back of the stove, a small piece of charred wood still smoldering.

"So this is where the wood goes," Addie murmured. She loaded it with another stick of wood, and even managed to stoke the flames from the ashes.

Then she lifted down an iron skillet from where it hung on the wall and loaded it with thick slices of bacon.

Now, feeling quite proud of her victory in figuring things out herself, she waited patiently for the stove to heat. She snooped around the rest of the kitchen and readied the plates, but ten minutes later, the bacon still looked as raw as when she had taken it out of the larder.

"Hmm." Addie tapped her bottom lip with her right index finger as she thought. Maybe the fire wasn't big enough to heat the pan and cook the bacon.

That must be it!

She added another thick stick of wood from the kindling box. Minutes later, the bacon was still white and pink, not at all ready to be eaten. Addie was beginning to lose confidence. Why wasn't it cooking? With tentative fingers, Addie touched the top of the stove to see if it was hot. It felt warm like before, but Josh would be eating raw bacon for dinner at this rate.

This is ridiculous! Addie thought. *I need to get the stove hotter!*

This time she added two large sticks of wood, filling the firebox to capacity.

Maybe if she twisted and turned the knobs, that might help as well. Sure enough, within minutes, the bacon had begun to hiss and pop, a lovely aroma spreading throughout the kitchen.

And to think, yesterday she had been concerned about learning to cook! No wonder her father had not instructed her tutors to teach her how to cook. This was simple.

Anyone could do it! It had taken a few tries with getting the right amount of wood to heat the stove properly, but she had figured it out relatively quickly, and all by herself!

Now she just needed to cook some eggs to accompany the bacon. She would really like to add biscuits to the menu, but she wasn't quite brave enough for that. She'd better save actual mixing and baking for at least lunch.

Returning to the larder, Addie took inventory of what was available, trying to get some ideas for lunch or dinner. However, though she could identify food items, she had no idea how one might prepare them. Finally giving up on inspiration, Addie decided to take things one meal at a time, and instead, took three eggs out of a bin on the shelf.

She sniffed the air. Something didn't smell right. If she didn't know any better, she would say the bacon was burning. But that was impossible. She had just checked it.

Holding two eggs in her left hand, and the third in her right, she hurried to the stove. Smoke spiraled up from the pan. The bacon was blackening at an alarming rate.

Addie frantically turned her head from side to side, searching the kitchen for a place to set the eggs. No time!

Transferring the third egg onto the palm of her left hand, she held all three eggs close to her body. With her right hand, she scraped the burned bacon frantically with a long wooden spoon.

Smoke billowed from the stove, burning Addie's eyes and causing them to water, clouding her vision. The acrid smell seared her throat.

What had she done? Sweat beaded on her forehead from the rising temperature. She looked around frantically, not knowing what to do to shut down the stove and stop the massive amount of smoke

The back door opened and a shouting Josh ran into the kitchen.

"The house is on fire!"

"No, just the bacon! Here, take these!" Addie passed Josh the eggs with a little too much force.

Time paused for one awful second as, horrified, Addie watched yellow yolks drip down the front of Josh's shirt.

With no time to apologize, Addie rushed back to the stove, crying "I have to get the bacon out of the pan!"

Just then the pot containing the remaining coffee boiled over.

Addie yelped in surprise, jumping back from the evil stove.

"Stand back!" Josh ordered, shoving her behind him. "The stove is too hot!" Grabbing an oven glove, Josh jerked open the firebox. "How much wood did you put in here? And the dampers are open all of the way! Were you trying to make the stove explode?"

Addie's chin quivered. "No, I was trying to cook you breakfast. I'm sorry. I'm not familiar with this type of stove." She wasn't familiar with any stove for that matter.

"If you don't know how to do something, just ask! Don't set the house on fire."

Josh twisted the dampers closed, then grabbed a pitcher full of water from the table and threw it on the flames.

Water hissed as it struck the hot surface. Thick smoke continued to pour out of the iron contraption from every opening, obscuring the charred remains of what once was bacon.

Josh stood straight and tall, his face blackened with ash, and egg running down his hands and shirt.

Not able to face the anger and disappointment she knew she would read in his eyes, Addie turned and ran. She fled the house, letting the screen door slam behind her. With tears streaming down her heated face, she ran with no destination.

She was humiliated. She was a fool to think she could impress Josh with her cooking.

With nowhere to go, she ran blindly. Everything was unfamiliar. Texas was so different than New York. She didn't belong on a ranch or in a kitchen. She belonged in a parlor, hosting dinner parties and having tea with the wives of her father's business partners.

Through blurry eyes, she saw a large wooden structure with a pitched roof. She slipped through a space in the front door and found the darkest corner she could. Stumbling into a dark stall, her back found a wall. She leaned against the wood planks for support, then with a shuddering breath, she slid to the hay-littered dirt floor.

She sobbed out her failure and frustration. "God help me!" she moaned desperately, but she knew she didn't deserve help. She had messed everything up far worse than almost burning down the house with the bacon. God had told Charlotte to be a mail order bride, and Addie had interfered with God's plans. Addie had stolen the man meant to be Charlotte's husband. Was she now being punished?

Addie breathed deeply, trying to calm her sobs and letting the familiar smells of horse and hay calm her. Her crying gradually reduced to hiccups, and she knew what she had to do. She didn't belong here. She had to tell Josh the truth.

The thought of admitting to Josh that she was an impostor terrified her, and yet, she felt a peace about her decision. Maybe God would forgive her if she tried to make amends.

As her emotions settled down, she gradually became more aware of her surroundings. At the sound of a soft nicker, she stretched her stiff muscles and crept out of the shadows.

The stable housed numerous stalls, all swept clean, with fresh hay piled neatly in the corners. But the stalls were empty. Addie assumed the horses must be in the corral, or being used by the ranch hands.

With the rippling sound of another hushed nicker, Addie knew that at least one horse remained in the barn.

"Well, hello there," Addie said quietly, arriving at the last stall in the row. A white mare stood at the back of the stall. Seeing that she measured just about as wide across as she was tall, Addie realized this was the horse Josh had mentioned last night.

"You must be Clementine." Addie scooped up a handful of oats from a barrel outside the stall door. "Here you go, Girl."

She stretched out her arm, palm up, inviting the horse to eat. Having grown up taking riding lessons, horses might be the only aspects of ranch life that Addie was remotely familiar and comfortable with, so she was eager to make friends.

But at her outstretched hand, Clementine tossed her head

wildly and kicked her rear legs against the back of the stall.

"It's okay, Clementine." Addie coaxed. "Wouldn't you like some oats?"

The mare neighed loudly, continuing to thrash her head. With her free hand, Addie reached further into the stall, attempting to calm Clementine with a touch to her black mane.

"I'd move my hand if I was you. She's liable to bite it off."

Addie started, dropping the oats onto the dirt floor.

A man with shoulder length black hair sticking out at odd angles from under a misshapen cowboy hat approached from the front of the stable.

Addie's hackles rose, the drama from earlier making her defensive. She might not know how to cook, but she knew how to ride a horse. "She won't bite me. Horses love me."

"Well, this one sure don't."

"And why would that be?" Addie snapped, her already irritated temper was beginning to boil over like the coffee pot.

This cowhand with the grizzled face and rustic deerskin breeches knew nothing about her. For some reason, all of Addie's emotion zeroed in on him, and she felt that, if the horse really didn't like her, then it was all his fault!

In spite of her gut reaction to stay and prove to the intruder that she really was good with horses, she moved away from the stall, giving the disgruntled horse some much needed space.

"Clementine is like most women I've met," the man drawled, indicating the horse with the tilt of his head. "She has the temper of a rattlesnake, and is as jealous as the day is long. I reckon you smell like Josh which makes her mighty mad. Just another reason why women should not be allowed to set foot on a ranch."

"You're Josh's uncle," Addie said in surprise.

She had thought this man with the wild hair and horrible taste in clothing was Hank, the ranch-hands cook, or even a drifter who had stumbled onto the Bar H, not an owner of one of the largest ranches in Texas. He definitely didn't look the part.

Normally Addie would have smiled and batted her lashes once she realized the man's importance, but for some reason she just couldn't bring herself to use her usual charm. Perhaps it was because this man knew she didn't belong in Texas. He had no illusions of who she was, or who she was pretending to be.

"Bad luck every last one of them," Pete continued, nodding his head for emphasis. He took Addie's place at Clementine's stall door. Immediately, the mare settled and nuzzled her head against Pete's shoulder.

Addie sighed heavily. "Josh told me you were against women being on a ranch."

"Yes, sirree. And I would hazard a guess that you might agree with my thoughts of women and ranchin' not mixing."

"What makes you say that?" Addie asked cautiously.

"Well, for starters, you are hiding in this here stable with a horse that clearly don't like you."

"And secondly?" Addie asked.

"Your eyes are red, and you have streaks of mud running down your face. If I didn't know better, I'd think you've been in the company of a large bottle of whisky. But since that don't seem likely, I'm guessin' that means you've been crying."

Addie hastily swiped at her cheeks. Her fingers came back blackened with soot. She must look a sight.

"I wasn't hiding."

"Could have fooled me. Where's your new husband?"

Addie's shoulders slumped in dejection. "In the kitchen."

"He's in the kitchen and you're in the barn. Seems like you've got your responsibilities reversed."

"I burned the bacon I was trying to cook."

"Is that what happened? Me and the cowhands saw smoke pourin' out of the kitchen, and Josh lit out of there for the house like a jackrabbit with his tail on fire."

Addie covered her face in mortification. She had hoped her cooking failure had been witnessed only by Josh. Apparently that was too much to hope for. Perhaps Pete was right. Women were very unlucky on this ranch.

"Well, speak of the devil," Pete said, looking at something over Addie's shoulder.

Addie turned. Josh stood looking more handsome than ever in a clean shirt and freshly scrubbed face. But he wasn't wearing his usual easy smile.

Was he angry with her?

Addie's chin quivered as she fought the tears that threatened to return.

"I wondered where you ran off to, Uncle Pete," Josh said, his eyes focused on the cowboy, as if Addie wasn't even there.

"I wasn't the one runnin,' boy," Pete grinned. He gave Clementine one last pat to her back. "I'll just be on my way now. Give you newlyweds some privacy. Say, how did that bacon taste, Josh? Fire-kissed?"

Pete chuckled all the way out the door while Josh's gaze swung to Addie the instant his uncle's back was turned. He stared at her for several minutes, his expression unreadable.

Addie twisted her hands, unable to take the silence any longer. "Josh, I'm sorry," Addie began.

"I'd like to take you on a picnic."

"A picnic?" Had she heard him correctly? Why wasn't he telling her to pack her bags and leave?

"Yes. I thought we could take a ride. I can show you the ranch, and then we can have an early dinner by the river."

"You don't want me to leave?"

Josh's forehead puckered. "Why would I want you to leave? You're my wife! Where did you get that idea?"

Before she could answer, a light dawned on his furrowed brow, then his eyes narrowed to slits as he asked warily. "Did Uncle Pete tell you to leave? What were you and Pete talking about?"

"Nothing in particular. Pete didn't say anything about me leaving. I just thought after what happened with the stove..." Addie's voice trailed off. "I really am sorry. Is the stove ruined?"

"No, it's fine," Josh waved his hand dismissively. "It's being cleaned up right now."

"By whom?"

"Hank."

"Oh." Addie continued to twist her hands. Another person who knew of her failures. The list grew by the minute. "A picnic and a tour sounds lovely. Thank you."

"I will be back this afternoon to pick you up. You can ride, can't you?"

"Yes." Addie said firmly. "Do you have a boy horse?"

"A boy horse?" he asked, his tone thoroughly confused.

"Yes. It appears that your female horses are in love with you and don't like the competition." Addie gestured to Clementine.

The horse seemed to glare at Addie.

Josh's lips lifted at the corners.

Addie found herself returning his smile, relieved that the tension from earlier was gone.

"I'll find you a boy horse."

"What about a picnic basket? I would be happy to cook—"

"No," Josh hurriedly cut her off, his eyebrows lifting in instant panic. "There's no need. I've already taken care of that as well. Just be ready to go around 3:00."

Josh left soon after, returning to his duties and leaving Addie no choice but to go back to the house.

In light of what happened earlier, she chose to enter the house through the front door. She held the screen, closing it softly so it didn't bang shut. She then crept quietly around to the stairs, giving the kitchen a wide berth, especially when she heard loud muttering about a "fool woman."

At the sound of the muttered insults, Addie's

anticipation for the picnic drained, leaving her weak as she trudged up the steps to the bedroom. It was just another reminder of what she had to do. The picnic was not to be a romantic respite with her husband, no matter how much she wanted to just forget everything and enjoy his company.

She didn't belong here. She had to confess.

Chapter 6

"WITH all of the excitement this morning, I never had the chance to tell you how beautiful you look in that dress."

Addie's cheeks warmed. "Thank you."

Josh's compliments only added to her delight. She didn't know if she had ever had a more enjoyable afternoon. Josh had gone out of his way to make it special. True to his word, he had arrived at the house with enough time to clean up and scrub off the dirt and grime of a hard day's work. Promptly at 3:00, he had descended the stairs in a clean shirt, smelling of fresh soap, his hair slightly damp.

He had selected a docile mare for her after all, but insisted that Betsy had no fondness for him at all. Addie had hoped for a stallion similar to Josh's horse, but she realized that she would have to prove herself before Josh trusted her with a more spirited mount. After all, he thought she could cook, and look how that had turned out.

They had ridden several miles while Josh pointed out various landmarks, explaining about the everyday operations of the Bar H. After the grand tour, Josh had circled back toward the ranch, to his favorite spot by the creek.

Together they had spread out a checkered blanket and unpacked a wicker basket that Josh had tied to his saddle.

"This food is wonderful. I think Hank is a better cook than you give him credit for," Addie said, having just finished eating a generous slice of cornbread. She was seriously contemplating a second serving. With its moist, crumbly center and lightly browned crust, it practically melted in your mouth.

Josh's eyes twinkled. "Hank didn't make the cornbread. I did."

Addie's eyebrows rose in surprise. "You can bake?"

"Yes. My mother taught me. I made this batch of cornbread for dinner the other day. Thankfully, it keeps well."

"Your mother must have been an amazing woman. Especially considering your uncle's standpoint on ranches and women." Addie had been puzzling over this conundrum all afternoon while she waited for their picnic. "Was she the exception to his rule?" She shot Josh a smile, "I know, her incredible cornbread must have won him over."

Josh shook his head and turned his gaze to the creek. "My mother is the reason Pete created his rule about women. Her cornbread never stood a chance."

Oh. Curiosity got the best of Addie, and she couldn't let Josh's silence be the last word. "Did they not get along?"

she prompted.

"The opposite actually." As if returning from his memories, Josh turned back to Addie, now speaking conversationally. "He and my father both loved her. She almost tore the Bar H apart, though it was no fault of her own. Two brothers in love with the same woman. It couldn't end well. And it didn't. My mother chose my father, and Pete left. In one day, Pete lost his brother, the woman he loved, and his ranch." Josh's voice faded and once again he stared off into the distance, his mind lost in the past.

"Did your parents ask Pete to leave?"

Josh glanced back at Addie, seemingly surprised by her question. "No, not at all. My father asked him to come back repeatedly. Pete finally did, but by then it was too late. I was still young, about fifteen. It was Spring, and my father and the ranch hands were on a cattle drive. A storm hit, and his horse spooked. He was thrown and trampled by the stampeding cattle. My mother sent a telegram to Pete. He arrived a few hours after my dad died, missing the opportunity to reconcile on this side of heaven. After the funeral, Pete stayed on to teach me everything I needed to know about ranching. I think he intended to only stay for a few months, but a few months turned to years, and by then, we had grown close. I probably reminded him of my father, and his presence helped ease some of the ache of losing my pa."

"What about your mother?" Addie asked quietly, lost in Josh's story. "Did Pete love her even after all of the years that had passed?"

"To the outside world, no. By then, he had adopted his views on women and ranches, became quite outspoken actually, and avoided my mother as much as possible. He built his cabin, and she stayed in the main house."

"So he hated her."

"Not really." Josh shook his head and idly threw a stick into the creek. "She believed he did, but Pete blamed himself for what happened. I think seeing her just reminded him of all that he had lost. He carried around a lot of guilt. Still does. He believes that if he had been there that night, my father wouldn't have been thrown from his horse and killed."

Addie sat still, watching the gentle flow of the creek, lost in the sad love story. She saw the trees hanging over the creek, sashaying their branches in the gentle breeze. She heard the trickling flow of the water over the rocks at the bank and felt the warmth of the descending sun.

But in her mind, she saw the story unfold as if on stage. She felt the sorrow of Pete's unrequited love, the tears of Josh's mother, torn between two brothers, and the grief of a pardon never received. Though she didn't even know these people, she still longed for the happy ending that never was.

"Do you think Pete still loved your mother?" she asked quietly

"Yes," Josh replied solemnly. "He cried when she died. I'd never seen him shed a tear before that day. Even at my father's funeral."

Addie felt like she understood Pete a little more, but she was still confused about how to merge the tragic figure in Josh's story with the rough, insulting cowboy from the barn. "So if this all was because of your mother, why does he still feel all women are bad luck?" Addie pointed out, thinking aloud. "After all, I don't think he's in danger of falling in love with me."

Josh threw back his head and laughed. "You're probably right. He doesn't like burned bacon. We're safe from history repeating itself. Pete will come around. Just give him time."

Josh picked up another slice of ham, and then turned his direct gaze to Addie. "What about your family, Addie? You didn't mention much in your letters about your father. Did he pass away when you were young?"

This was the moment Addie had been dreading. She could lie and say, 'yes,' which would probably halt Josh from questioning her further, but he had been so open with her about his family's tumultuous past. And she had vowed that she would tell him the truth. They could never have a real relationship if she kept living a lie. Taking a deep breath, Addie began.

"My father and I never got along," she admitted. "He was disappointed that I was a girl. He wanted a son badly, but after I was born, the doctor warned my parents that my mother should not have any more children. But my mother loved my father, and saw how much my father longed for a son. They were both so happy when, years later, she was expecting another child. They were convinced it was their long-awaited boy. I was ten at the time. Those few months were the happiest of my childhood. But it didn't last. The doctor had been correct. The baby was born too soon, and both my mother and my baby sister died."

Addie waited with baited breath. Any moment Josh would realize that what Addie had just told him did not match up to what Charlotte, his real mail-order bride, had written in her letters.

She breathed deeply, waiting, yet trying to keep up the courage to face what came ahead.

Josh's eyes remained fixed on a spot on the blanket next to Addie.

She felt a sting on her back, and wondered if a thread had come loose on her dress. She felt a similar sharp sting on her leg, but she tried not to get distracted from what she knew she must do. At the prick of a third sting on her hip, she reached to scratch it, doggedly plowing forward despite Josh's silence and apparent disinterest.

"Josh, I am not—"

Addie watched as Josh's gaze moved slowly from the blanket, up her skirt, to the bodice of her dress.

Addie's fingers absently scratching her hip suddenly met with multiple stings like a firecracker going off.

She gasped in pain, even as she saw Josh's eyes widen.

Josh jumped to his feet. In one swift motion, he scooped Addie up from the blanket, ran the few steps to the river bank, and threw her into the water.

Addie landed in the creek with a splash. Silt and muddy water filled her mouth. Coughing, Addie sputtered. "Why did you do that?"

"Get further into the river!" Josh barked.

Did he really hate her that much that he was trying to drown her?

"You're covered in ants!" he shouted.

"Wh-what!" Addie stumbled backward into the water. Her head completely submerged. Finding her footing, she shot back up, sputtering and wiping at her face.

Her vision cleared just in time to see Josh jump and swat furiously at his shoulder with his hand. Then his feet started pumping, as if he was dancing a jig. Meanwhile, his hands widened their territory and looked to be swiping down his body from head to toe.

Seeming to finally admit defeat, Josh yelped and ran headlong into the creek.

Addie jumped aside as he came barreling in, again losing her footing and sinking into the murk. She surfaced only to realize she'd lost her grip on the muddy ground and was now caught in the deepest part of the creek. Her boots kicked back and forth, not finding anything but water. She leaned back, kicking hard to keep her head above water, but the weight of her dress and petticoats kept pulling her back down.

She yelled for Josh, but water filled her mouth. She gagged, struggling for air. Her head surfaced, only as her strangled gasp earned her another mouthful of water.

And she was down again, deeper than before, the weight of her dress dragging her to meet the creek's soggy floor.

Dear God, help me! She prayed frantically. Was this how she was going to die? Tormented by ants, then drowned in a heavily petticoated, stolen green dress?

Strong arms surrounded her, lifting her back up to air and sunshine. She gasped, frantically wrapping her arms tightly around her rescuer's neck.

"I can't breathe, Addie!" Josh squawked.

Addie loosened her hold only slightly, terrified he would let her go.

Apparently he managed to get just enough air and began kicking them both toward shore.

Addie tucked her head close to his neck and shut her

eyes, hoping Josh was a strong enough swimmer to save them both.

She felt the instant Josh's weight shifted and his feet found the bottom of the creek. Yet she remained with head planted close to Josh, too terrified to move.

"You're safe now, Addie. You're fine," he crooned softly. "I'm not going to let you go."

Though Addie was sure she could now stand in the more shallow water, Josh still held her securely in his arms, and she was thankful. With one of his arms now at her back and the other under her legs, she was completely cradled against his chest.

She leaned her head against him, closing her eyes and letting the sound of his heartbeat soothe her and the feel of his strong arms protect her.

After several minutes, the soft lapping of the water and the cooing of birds in the trees had calmed her enough that she opened her eyes, only to find Josh steadily gazing back at her.

She locked eyes with him, neither looking away.

"I'm sorry I threw you in the creek," Josh said seriously.

"It was better than being eaten by ants," Addie replied.

"Well, they wouldn't have eaten you. They just—"

"Sting." Addie finished. "Horribly."

"Did you get stung?" Josh asked, concerned and looking her over for signs of trauma.

"Yes, but I think I'll be okay, provided that the rest of the ants in my dress are sufficiently drowned."

"We need to get you back to the house," Josh said. "The

temperature will be dropping soon, and I need to make sure you aren't hurt worse."

"I would have been, if you hadn't saved me," Addie said seriously, looking back up into his wet face.

Josh finally let her feet slide down to meet the muddy bottom of the creek, but he kept both his arms around her, holding her steady as she leaned against his chest for support.

Gazing into his handsome face, Addie watched the drops of water drip off his dark hair and trail down the masculine planes of his face. His eyes looked a slightly darker blue than before, and she now noticed that they were framed by long, dark eyelashes that held tiny beads of moisture.

She felt Josh reach up and draw his finger across her cheek.

"An ant?" she questioned, wondering if he'd just saved her again from one last rogue villain intending to do her harm.

The corners of Josh's mouth lifted up in a quiet smile. "No," he whispered.

His finger swept under her chin, tilting up her face slightly to meet his. Then his lips reached down to caress her cheek with a gentle kiss, right where his finger had been.

"Not an ant," he whispered.

Carefully, he placed another gentle kiss on her other cheek.

"Not an ant," he repeated.

Her forehead.

"Not an ant."

Finally, he paused, a fraction above her lips.

His husky voice barely audible, he breathed, "Not an ant."

His lips met hers in a soft caress. Addie's breath caught, and she wasn't sure she ever wanted to breathe again. His kiss was sweet, not at all demanding, and yet it held the promise of something deep and passionate.

It wasn't a short kiss, but it wasn't long either. Before Addie was ready, his lips were gone and she was looking back up into his warm eyes.

Would it be improper for her to wrap her arms around his neck and pull him back for a repeat?

"Let's get you home," Josh said, quickly lifting her into his arms to carry her from the creek.

He trudged forward, and Addie knew with her water-soaked dress and petticoats, she had to rival the pregnant Clementine for weight.

When they were almost to shore, Addie saw something in her field of vision just past Josh's shoulder.

"Oh, Josh, it's your hat!" She said, pointing to where it floated in the shallow water.

Josh set her down carefully in the ankle deep water and slogged through the murk to retrieve his hat.

With his back turned, Addie somehow managed to bend down in her stiff, soaked garments. When Josh turned and sloshed back her direction, she was ready.

Aiming directly at Josh, she pushed the water in one mighty splash. Startled, Josh stood there frozen in place, as once again, he got completely soaked.

"What was that for?" he asked, finally finding his voice.

Addie stepped smartly out of the water with as much poise as she could and headed for her horse, Betsy. Over her shoulder, she called innocently.

"Don't worry. It was not an ant!"

Chapter 7

"YOU want me to kill... a chicken... with that?" Addie asked, pointing to the wicked looking metal object that Josh held in one hand. It was the morning after their ant picnic, and Addie had been drinking a cup of lukewarm coffee alone in the kitchen, when Josh had opened the back door and walked in with an axe in tow. Addie's stomach had dropped instantly, knowing no good could come from this conversation. He had announced that today was the day she would win Pete over with a chicken dinner.

"Yes. Just cut off his head, pluck out the feathers and cook him for dinner."

"Kill the chicken."

"Yes."

"With an axe."

"Yes."

"Just chop off his head."

"That's right."

Addie felt all the blood drain from her face. Was she going to faint? Addie sat down heavily into a wooden chair, her cup landing on the kitchen table with a heavy thud.

Josh leaned the axe against the wall, concern lining his handsome features.

"Are you alright?

"Yes. I'm fine." She wasn't really. The few sips of coffee she drank threatened to make a reappearance.

"Are the ant bites hurting you? If you don't feel up to this, we can wait a few days."

Yes! Addie began to nod her head vigorously.

"I just thought you might want to have another go at cooking now that I showed you how to use the stove. You said in your letters that fried chicken and biscuits were your specialty."

Charlotte.

Addie's head stopped moving as Josh continued. "You even mentioned winning a contest. You said you had to pluck chickens for a week straight, practicing so you could perfect your recipe. Do you remember asking me to excuse your poor handwriting because your fingers were stiff from plucking feathers? Ever since then, I've been dreaming of tasting this prizewinning fried chicken."

Good grief! Where did Charlotte grow up that killing and plucking chickens was an everyday occurrence? Oh, right. Atlanta. Addie felt a grudging respect for the girl whose ticket she had stolen.

"Could you kill the chicken?" Addie asked in a small voice, looking at him through lowered eyelashes in what she hoped resembled a demure appeal to the heroic cowboy.

"I can't," he said, her plea not even fazing him. Instead, he looked out the window as if he really needed to be somewhere else. "I have to ride out now with several of the ranch hands to check on our herd in the south forty. Clint saw some men he didn't recognize riding through those parts yesterday. I won't be back until supper. Would you like me to ask Pete to kill the chicken for you? He's fixing the corral today, so he will be sticking close to the house."

Addie found herself shaking her head again. No, definitely not Pete. He already disliked her. She needed to win him over by showing him what an asset she was to the ranch, not give him more evidence to strengthen his convictions.

"I can handle it," Addie said firmly, thankful that her voice didn't waver. If Charlotte could kill a chicken and pluck its feathers out, she could as well. She would worry about the cooking part later. Addie straightened her spine, her steely resolve returning.

With a much too quick kiss to her forehead and a whispered goodbye, Josh left, letting the screen door shut behind him like the bang of a judge's gavel. Addie had been hoping for a bit more along the lines of the kiss they had shared in the river.

With much trepidation, Addie lifted the axe from where Josh had left it. It weighed more she expected. Josh had made it look light when he had held it loosely with one hand. Setting her mouth firmly, she hefted the axe and headed out the door.

Might as well get it over with.

She had to use both hands to carry it as she marched across the front yard to the chicken coop Josh had shown her yesterday before they had ridden out on their tour.

The coop was built like a small cabin. It boasted exposed wood logs and nest boxes perched outside, held up by wooden stilts. The coop was situated not far from the corral. She could see Pete with his back to her, hammering some boards that had fallen down.

"I can do this, I can do this, I can do this," Addie chanted with each step she took. One look at the chickens milling around plucking at the feed on the ground had Addie changing her tune. "I can't do this. I can't do this. This is crazy! I'm not Charlotte."

Guilt rose in Addie's spirit. This charade was spinning out of control. Josh had apparently not heard her partial confession last night. He had made no mention of what she had spoken of seconds before the ant attack. Drat those ants! Every time she tried to be honest, circumstances arose that prevented her from revealing the truth.

What would happen if Charlotte made her way to Last Chance and the Bar H before Addie had a chance to tell Josh the truth? Where was Charlotte now? Was she still stuck in St. Louis?

"Stop. You can't think about that now." Addie scolded herself. "No time for guilt. You've got a chicken to kill."

The rest of this mess could be dealt with later. Over fried chicken. And biscuits.

Addie studied the chickens for several minutes, trying to

decide the best way to approach the situation. First, she had to catch the chicken. Then she would have to hold him down to, well, for lack of better words, take care of business.

A plump white rooster with black tail feathers ventured a little farther away from the others, its yellow beak to the ground.

Addie approached cautiously, lifting the axe to hold it like a club. She wet her suddenly dry lips. "Here, little chicken. Stay still please," she whispered softly, her heart racing.

Not wanting to scare him, Addie knelt down in the dirt and slowly shuffled forward on her knees. She was close now, and she could see the individual feathers on the chicken's neck ruffle in the slight breeze.

The rooster paused its eating. Addie held her breath as its black beady eyes stared her down.

The chicken held so still. Maybe she wouldn't have to catch him and hold him down. If she angled the axe just right, the deed could be done.

Releasing her breath, Addie closed her eyes. She raised the axe over her head. With a prayer to God that the chicken wouldn't suffer, she swung.

A loud squawk, and wild movement next to her skirts made Addie shudder.

She had done it!

She opened her left eye slowly, wary of what she would see. The bird had vanished. All that remained were a few black and white feathers stuck under the blade of the axe, littering the ground where the chicken once stood.

What happened? She was sure she had hit the chicken.

Confused, Addie stood and turned a slow circle, searching for her missing rooster.

He was easy to spot. He was the only chicken missing his tail-feathers. He stood alone next to the coop angrily pecking at the ground as his comrades continued to eat, oblivious to the drama surrounding them.

Addie stood, frustrated that she would have to try again. She thought about trying to catch a different chicken, but she was stubborn. She wouldn't give up easily. She had picked her chicken, and she was sticking with it. It had become a battle of wills now.

She approached slowly. The chicken scratched his toes in the dirt, like a bull pawing the earth before he charged. Addie stepped forward, letting the axe fall to the ground behind her. She would come back for it. She was going to need two hands for this.

She hunched down, determining the best course of action was to tackle the thing. She took a step closer.

The rooster tossed his head to the right and left warning her to stay back.

Another step forward.

The chicken flew straight at Addie's head.

She threw up her hands to shield her face.

It's red comb and wattle shook angrily as the enraged rooster launched itself at her repeatedly, using its wings to beat her furiously.

This chicken was attacking her, not the other way around!

The pins holding Addie's bun sprung free. Her thick

blonde hair cascaded down her back.

Addie felt her temper rising.

She grabbed the rooster's quivering body and yanked him off her face. Holding him at arm's length, he continued to struggle, desperately trying to peck at her with his beak. All around her chickens flew about, feathers and dust coating the air. Paying them no heed, Addie hugged the rooster to her chest, trying to avoid his sharp claws and beak.

The rooster made one last lunge at her face. She tried to back away, losing her balance and falling on her rear. The rooster jerked, and Addie barely held on with her fingertips. She rolled, pinning the chicken between her legs to get a better grip. Looking up, she saw the axe standing upright in the dirt, its blade embedded in the ground and gleaming as if struck by a sunbeam.

Still on her knees, Addie surged forward, the fingertips of one hand stretching to grasp the wooden handle of the axe.

Got it!

Blowing errant strands of hair out of her face, Addie stumbled to her feet, the quivering chicken in one hand, the axe dragging behind her in the other. She spotted a wooden stump next to the coop.

Forming a plan in her mind, Addie avoided the chickens that scrambled for the safety of the chicken coop. She held the chicken's round body firmly between her knees, his hocks and shanks kicking wildly.

"Almost there," she encouraged herself. She saw two nails stuck into the head of the stump. Perfect. Just what she needed. She secured the angry chicken's head between the nails, absently noting the numerous scratches on her hands.

Once that was done, she threw her mass of tangled blonde hair over her shoulder so she could better see what she was doing. Firmly grasping the handle, Addie lifted the axe up above her head.

Right as she had the axe at its peak, ready to swing down, the rooster broke free of the nails holding him down, once again flying straight at Addie. She let out a piercing scream and dropped the axe, folding her hands in front of her to protect her face.

Yet the squawking beast kept coming.

Addie backed away, stumbling and landing on the ground. Taking advantage of his fallen opponent, the rooster started at her feet and began pecking up her legs. Addie scrambled up once more and ran, tripping over her skirt in her haste.

But the chicken caught her, landing on her back and plucking out her hair. She swung at him repeatedly, shrieking the entire time. Finally Addie resorted to spinning round and round as fast as she could, and the rooster flew off. Now dizzy and fumbling for her footing, Addie ran for the house.

But she could hear the squawking bird still on her heels.

So frantic and traumatized, the only thing she could even manage to pray was a desperate, *Help!*

Just when she felt like she'd never escape, a large blur stepped past her and grabbed her adversary.

Addie stopped, practically falling over in exhaustion as she watched Pete walk over to a nearby stump and pin the rooster down.

"Fool woman!" Pete exclaimed, glaring at her. "I'll get the axe. All you have to do is watch him!"

Addie stumbled over to see her nemesis pinned securely to the stump. For once, he was still, as if all the fight had finally left him. His beady eyes stared at her while his scrawny little legs twitched.

Addie knew when she'd been bested.

Before she could think about the consequences, she bent over and with shaking hands, she released the rooster.

As the chicken's pointed toes hit the dirt, he paused, looking back at Addie, as if daring her to make another charge.

But Addie was done.

Now victorious and docile, the rooster scurried away and up into the safety of his coop kingdom.

"What are you doing, woman?" Pete's voice boomed from behind her.

Addie turned to see the large man glaring at her with the axe at his side.

"That bird fought and earned his freedom. I won't let it be taken from him."

"That's fine and dandy if you want to petition for chicken independence and starve yourself, but what are Josh and I supposed to eat for dinner?"

"Bacon," Addie retorted, swishing her dirty skirts as she marched past the man to tend to her war wounds. "I'll burn you some bacon!"

Chapter 8

"I didn't kill the chicken," Addie announced as soon as Josh walked through the kitchen door.

"I know," Josh said solemnly.

Pete.

Addie felt tears burning behind her eyes. Pete had obviously tattled before she'd had the chance to confess. Who knew what the crank had said about her.

Addie waited for the inevitable questions.

But Josh didn't ask any. In fact, he wouldn't even look at her. He silently hung his hat on a peg and immediately began preparing to make dinner.

Addie watched in helpless guilt as he took out a pot, filled it with water, and began assembling a stew.

"Please, Josh, let me help," she begged. She couldn't bear to watch him perform a task that was supposed to be her responsibility.

"No, Addie. If you want, you can set the table. But other than that, I think you've done enough already."

He was mad.

Sniffing back tears, Addie searched the cupboards, finding plates, glasses, and utensils to set the worn wood table. She didn't dare risk asking Josh where any of the supplies were, but eventually managed to do it herself.

When she finished and Josh still wasn't speaking to her, she walked outside and clipped some daisies from the front flower bed. Unable to find a vase of any kind, she filled a jar with water, stuck the flowers in, and set them in the middle of the table.

It made a pitiful contribution. She had hoped that the flowers would brighten the tense, depressing atmosphere. Maybe if Josh saw her making an effort, then he would talk to her again. But instead, the flowers looked forlorn in the middle of the table, like they didn't belong—just like her.

Apparently, Addie's husband didn't like to talk when he was upset, but Addie didn't know if she could handle that. As the minutes wore on, she grew more agitated. She needed to tell him what had happened, needed to confess everything, but he didn't seem to even want to listen. Should she just pack her trunk up and ask to be taken back to the train?

But the memory of their kiss in the river held her in place. He had liked her. And she liked him way too much to walk away. She only hoped she hadn't ruined everything with the chicken incident.

Uncertain, she watched as Josh peeled potatoes and carrots, then plopped them into the water on the stove.

That was something she could manage, she thought to herself. Whether or not Josh asked for it, she suddenly decided that she was going to help.

Retrieving a knife and sneaking away a few potatoes, Addie stationed herself at the table and began to peel a potato. With intense concentration, she made a long thin peel, then another, then—

"Addie, I already have enough potatoes," Josh said, right behind her shoulder.

At the sound of his voice, she lost her hold on the potato. She tried to grip it tighter, but her fingers slid over the slippery surface and launched the potato into the air like from a cannon. The potato found its mark, landing squarely on the glass jar of flowers with a force that broke the glass, spilling flowers and water all over.

Josh grabbed some towels and together they mopped up the mess, but by the time the unfortunate daisies had been disposed of, Addie was mopping her tears off the table as well.

"I'm sorry, Josh," she said brokenly. "I know I seem to say that a lot. But I am sorry. About the jar and the flowers. About the chicken. About my cooking. If you would just let me explain."

"Fine. Tell me about the chicken."

Though he had finally given her permission, his tone sounded flat, like he didn't really care what she said. He'd already found her guilty.

Nevertheless, Addie plunged in. "I'm sorry I couldn't kill Patrick, Josh. I just couldn't do it. I tried, but he fought so hard—"

"Patrick? Who's Patrick?" Josh asked, scratching his head in confusion.

"The rooster. Patrick Henry."

"You named the rooster?" Josh groaned, shutting his eyes and sinking down into a chair at the table. "Please tell me you didn't name the rooster."

"Well, I didn't intend to," Addie explained quickly. "But he fought so hard to get away that he kind of reminded me of a patriot. Then somehow, in my mind, he became Patrick Henry. I didn't really name him; it just sort of happened."

Josh groaned again, "And of course, you had to pick the meanest rooster we have to go after. Why couldn't you have killed one of the hens?"

"I didn't know I was supposed to kill a certain one," Addie explained, slightly indignant. "Patrick Henry was just the first one I spotted. Next time you need to be a little more clear in your instructions."

Josh sighed, rubbing a hand down the front of his face, as if in frustration. "I have to make the cornbread," he said, standing and turning away from her.

"Josh, show me how to do it," Addie begged, following him to where he set a large bowl on the counter. "If you tell me what to do, I can learn. Then I'll be able to do it myself."

"That's what I don't understand, Addie," Josh said, turning to her with the first visible signs of anger. "I don't care that you didn't kill the chicken. If you didn't want to, that's fine. What I don't understand is how you told me all these things in your letters that now seem to have been lies. You told me you knew how to cook. You told me your specialty was fried chicken and that you'd killed and prepared the chickens yourself. Why should I have to teach you to cook, unless every word you told me in your letters was a lie?

"Josh, please let me explain," Addie said desperately. She hated having him mad at her. It felt even worse knowing that she deserved every bit of his anger.

"What can you possibly say to explain deceiving me? Pete told me it was a mistake to get a mail order bride. But I assured him that you could hold your own on our ranch—that you would make great contributions. Now you can't cook, refuse to kill a chicken for our dinner, and then name that dinner and make him your pet! However, all of that I could deal with if I had just known the real Addie. It's the lying I find inexcusable. I thought you'd be more than a pretty face."

His words felt like she was being slapped repeatedly with a whip. She worked to swallow the lump in her throat and control the tears that made her breathing ragged.

Now was the time to tell the truth. After all, there was no possible way he could think worse of her than he already did.

"Josh, I didn't lie, but I did deceive you. You see, I am not—"

The door creaked open and Pete walked in. "The house isn't afire, so I assume Josh is the one cooking tonight."

Completely oblivious, Pete took a chair at the table, laced his hands behind his head, and leaned the chair back on two legs. "Smells like stew. Are you making cornbread to go with it?"

"Yes," Josh replied, immediately retreating from the standoff with Addie.

While Pete launched into a monologue on the fencing repairs being done on the east property line, Addie watched carefully as Josh measured the ingredients for cornbread.

Suddenly, Josh turned and handed her the spoon. "Stir it up and then we'll put it in the pan."

Thankful to have something useful to do, Addie whipped the spoon around the bowl, vigorously launching a hunk of batter onto her cheek. Hoping Josh and Pete were too engrossed in their conversation to notice, she reached up and removed the evidence, then returned to her task of stirring, this time at a much slower pace.

She hadn't been paying attention to their conversation, but she tuned in just as they were discussing plans for the next day.

"It's going to be a long day in the saddle tomorrow," Pete said, clearly not looking forward to it.

"Yes, but there's no way to avoid it," Josh replied. "The cattle have to be moved to new pastures. And with rustlers reported in the area, I want them all moved away from the property borders."

"Long day tomorrow?" Addie asked, unable to ignore the conversation and its potential effect on her.

Josh turned. "Yes, I wanted to tell you. We'll leave early in the morning and be gone all day until evening. I'm sorry to leave you alone, but we don't really have a choice."

Addie nodded, trying to show confidence she didn't feel,

"Don't worry about me. I'll be fine."

Pete stood to his feet and spoke up. "One good thing about being gone all day, Josh, is that you won't have to risk your life with your wife's cooking!"

Chuckling at his own humor, Pete announced he was off to visit the 'apple knocker' and stepped out the door, presumably to use the outhouse.

Once he left, silence again descended on the kitchen. Addie focused on stirring the yellow mixture in the bowl, wondering how she was supposed to know when it was ready to go in the pan.

She somehow felt the warmth of Josh's presence behind her, even before he touched her. His hand came around and enfolded hers as it grasped the spoon. With strong, even strokes, he guided her hand in stirring the cornbread. He stood so close behind her that she found herself leaning in to his solid chest, feeling the whisper of his breath against her ear.

"I'm sorry I got angry, Addie," Josh said quietly. "I know you have a good explanation for things, and I want to hear it."

The spoon in the bowl stopped stirring and Addie turned her palm up to lace Josh's fingers with hers. She didn't know if she would ever find the right words to soften the truth, and the more she struggled with it, the more difficult it became.

"Addie, what are these?" Josh said before Addie could speak.

At Josh's alarmed tone, Addie looked down to see her scratched-up hand in his. Without waiting for permission,

Josh slid the sleeve of her dress up, revealing the angry, red scratches extending past where he could see.

"Addie, you're hurt!" Josh exclaimed. "What happened?"

"Patrick Henry," Addie said simply. "I really tried to kill him, but he bested me. I'm alright though. Just a few scratches here and there, nothing major."

Josh suddenly looked ill. "Addie, I didn't know. Pete told me he was going to kill the chicken and you wouldn't let him."

"Well, that's true," Addie said.

"But obviously not the whole story."

"Is that cornbread ready yet?" Pete asked, letting the door swing shut behind him.

At his uncle's entrance, Josh let Addie go.

"Not quite," Addie said, recovering quickly and spooning the batter into the prepared pan.

While Josh opened the oven door, she slid it inside.

"Now, Josh, why did you do that?" Pete questioned. "She touched it, now I don't know if it will be edible."

"Then don't eat it," Josh snapped.

Pete raised his eyebrows at his nephew's tone, but didn't say anything.

What followed was one of the most unpleasant evenings of Addie's life. Though Josh had spoken sharply to his uncle, his anger didn't last long. Soon they were talking and laughing over the stew and cornbread, effectively blocking Addie out of all conversation.

Addie's feelings of loneliness only intensified as the men retired to the porch after dinner. She guessed they thought cleaning and dishes were safe for her to figure out on her own. But by the time everything was done, she was crying in pain. The soap and water irritated the cuts on her hands. And the other cuts all over her body were not painless either.

Thankfully, her face had been spared, all except a long gash down her neck. After cleaning up from the battle, Addie had found salve for her cuts, then strategically arranged her hair so that Josh wouldn't notice the injury.

But now she felt every single cut made by Patrick Henry's beak. Her head also hurt where he'd plucked out her hair. Addie had unfortunately discovered that a little chicken beak can go a long way. She literally hurt from head to toe. Not to mention, she still had painful, itchy spots from the ant attack the day before.

All in all, she was absolutely miserable as she climbed up the stairs. She hastily readied for bed and slid between the sheets. But sleep was elusive.

She tried to pray, but couldn't even manage that. God remained as silent as ever. Not that Addie blamed Him. She was the one who had messed things up. And yet, she couldn't help but long to be like Charlotte. Having the comfort of God's voice seemed like an unreachable treasure.

Josh eventually came to bed, but Addie held still, pretending to be asleep. She didn't feel like talking, especially with tears streaming down her face. Luckily, Josh's breathing evened out quickly, and Addie didn't have to work so hard to keep the sobs in.

She cried in pain and frustration. She cried because she

was alone and couldn't hear God. She also cried because she knew she would never be able to earn Josh's love.

But mostly, she cried because she didn't belong.

Chapter 9

THE next night, Addie prepared for bed in an eerily quiet and empty house. It was dark outside now, approaching midnight.

The sun had set, and Josh, Pete, and the other ranch hands had yet to return. Addie prayed they hadn't run into trouble with cattle rustlers. Or that a stampede hadn't occurred like when Josh's father died. Addie's anxious worries caused her to search the horizon often to see if she could spot the riders returning home.

Addie changed into Charlotte's cotton nightgown, and brushed her hair. She felt tired, more so than usual after sleeping fitfully the night before. After crying herself to sleep, Josh's disappointed face had haunted her dreams.

She had awoken when Josh quietly collected his clothing to ready for the day. She hadn't said a word, even though she desperately wanted to. And he hadn't placed his customary goodbye kiss to her forehead.

All day Addie had tried to keep busy, dusting and sweeping, cleaning as best as she could. She desperately wanted to be a help around the ranch and prove herself, but feared she might do more harm than good. Catastrophes seemed to fall in her wake.

She had skipped breakfast and lunch, her appetite non-existent. For dinner, she had carefully arranged the wood in the stove like Josh had taught her, heating last night's leftover stew. She hoped that Josh would arrive in time to eat dinner with her, but it was to no avail. She forced herself to swallow a few bites of stew and cornbread while she stood at the kitchen wash basin. She would be no use to Josh if she fainted or became ill from not eating properly.

With a tired sigh, Addie now climbed into bed. She rolled over to her side, praying for Josh's safe return. With how exhausted she was, she expected to fall asleep easily, but ten minutes later, she was still wide awake.

For some odd reason, she felt an inexplicable urge to go to the stable and check on Clementine. This was absurd. After eating her lonely dinner, Addie had gone to check on the horse, knowing that Clementine was due to foal any day now. Fresh hay and water lined the walls of the stall. The ranch hands had clearly prepared for the possibility of a late return.

Tiptoeing through the barn, Addie had heard Clementine snorting and pacing. She realized that despite her caution, Clementine must be aware of her presence.

"Calm down, Clementine," Addie said, backing away from the stall as soon as she arrived. "There is no need to kick yourself. I'm leaving." Addie left the stable, the sound of Clementine's kicks fading.

Now, less than an hour later, Addie's thoughts were preoccupied with the horse.

Addie rolled onto her back, staring at the dark ceiling. She couldn't shake the feeling that something was wrong with Clementine.

"She's fine. You just saw her," Addie reassured herself. She was being ridiculous. She was not going to march out to the stable in her nightclothes just so that Clementine could snort and kick her stall at her. Absolutely not. Never.

Five minutes later, Addie threw off her covers. "Oh, alright!" she moaned, reaching for her wrapper. Tying it securely about her waist, she then lit the oil lamp.

One quick peek at Clementine, and it was back to bed. Hopefully Josh would be home by then. The thought spurred her to action.

The kitchen door slammed shut as Addie walked quickly toward the stable, the hand holding the oil lamp trembling slightly. A flash of lightning lit the sky, followed by the distinct rumble of thunder. A storm was coming. The air felt cooler now than when she made her last trip to the stable. The wind had picked up, bringing along with it the scent of rain.

"Lord, please keep Josh and the others safe. Help them to come home quickly before the storm breaks," Addie prayed quietly. Speaking out loud made her feel slightly less alone. Darkness enveloped the ranch, the occasional slash of lightning brightening her path.

Addie reached the stable, grateful for its close proximity to the house. She didn't know if she would be as brave to complete her midnight errand if the stable was any farther away.

She held her lantern high above her head. The flame flickered as she tiptoed into the quiet, hesitant to disturb the cantankerous horse if she slept. A muffled noise came from the back of the stable. Clementine must be awake after all.

The light from her lamp illuminated a small patch of the interior of the stall. Addie expected to see Clementine standing, ready to nip her at first sight.

Instead, the horse lay on the ground on her side, her body a ghostly white in the dark shadows of the stall. Was she sleeping? The noise came again.

Addie hesitated. She knew better than to open the stall door and enter. Clementine could stand up in a second, delivering a swift kick with her strong hooves. She might look docile now, but Addie had seen her teeth and the strength of her legs, especially when agitated.

Forgoing opening the stall, Addie searched the dark recesses of the stable for something to stand on to get a better look. Light from the oil lamp revealed a wooden milking stool perched at the end of the row of stalls.

Positioning the stool in front of Clementine's door, Addie hung the lantern on a hook above the stall and climbed on the stool, precariously balancing on the thin legs as she leaned her upper body over the wooden door. She stretched as far as she could without her feet going over her head. Once she reassured herself that Clementine was alive and well, she would run back to the house, her conscience clear, putting her silly premonitions to rest.

The glow of light revealed Clementine's swollen belly. The horse's quivering flanks were covered in sweat.

Clementine was definitely not sleeping. Clementine was in labor.

Addie's heart began to pound. What should she do? Oh, how she wished Josh was here! Really, anyone other than just her.

Clementine began grunting. It was a sound that Addie had heard before. Should she venture into the stall or wait?

Clementine's grunts became louder. Was the foal coming now? Addie strained to see.

Her breath caught, and her eyes widened.

Without a second thought, Addie jumped off her perch, and ran out of the barn. Cold rain immediately soaked her nightgown. She strained to see through the sheets of rain, but she could barely see the house. Lightning flashed, but even in the split second of illumination, she didn't see any riders. Thunder cracked on the heels of the lightning, and Addie ducked back inside.

She was alone. No one was going to come to Clementine's rescue. No one but her.

She ran back to the stall and jerked open the door, toppling the stool she had been standing on.

She stood there, completely soaked and breathing heavily, watching the mare with wide, terrified eyes. She knew Clementine and her foal wouldn't make it unless she did something.

She reached for the lamp and set it on the dirt floor.

Come on, Addie! she urged herself. *You can do this. All of those years spent in the stable back home have to be good for something!*

Knowing she didn't have a moment to waste, Addie

untied her wrap and threw it unheeded behind her. Next, she pushed the puffed sleeves of her nightgown up to her elbows.

Kneeling next to Clementine, Addie spoke softly, "Hi, there, Clementine. It's Addie. I'm going to help you."

She brought the lamp closer. It was worse than she had thought. From the door, she had seen that something was not right. Now she saw what should have been a gray-white sack emerging from the horse was instead brick-red. If the birth wasn't progressing in the right order, Addie knew the foal might not be getting oxygen. She knew enough to recognize that the foal should be coming first, but instead, it looked like the placenta had detached prematurely and was being delivered before the foal. If Addie didn't hurry, the foal could suffocate within minutes.

She had to get the foal out now.

Addie frantically searched the stall for something that she could use to puncture the sack. It needed to be sharp, but at the same time it couldn't injure the foal. Remembering the stool, Addie ran to the stall door. Rotating the stool onto its side, she brought the heel of her boot down heavily onto the top rung.

A satisfying, "Crack!" accompanied the rung snapping beneath her heel.

Armed now with her wooden stake, Addie returned to the stall.

With deft movements, Addie used the jagged stool leg on the red bag protruding from Clementine. Her hands steady, she reached into the mare with her left hand and felt for the water bag. Grasping it firmly, she cut through that bag as well.

Tossing her "tool" over her shoulder, Addie felt with her hands for the front hooves of the foal.

"Got them." Addie breathed. "Almost there, little guy. Hold on."

Working on her hands and knees, Addie pulled slightly. She could see the tips of his legs now! Staggering the legs as to not hurt Clementine, so one was delivered first, Addie gave one more large pull downward, and the rest of the foal followed.

With a grunt Addie landed backward in the dirt, a mass of brown legs and goo in her lap.

The foal began to gurgle. Addie reached for her wrap and frantically wiped at the moisture around the foal's nostrils. After several tense seconds, the foal began to breathe normally.

Addie heaved a great sigh of relief. She laid the foal next to its mother. Clementine raised her head and began nuzzling her foal.

Tears prickled Addie's eyes. Completely exhausted, she fell back into the hay. There had been no time to panic before, but now her adrenaline wore off. She suddenly felt very lightheaded, and her hands began to shake.

"Addie?" a frantic voice boomed.

Josh.

"In here," she called weakly.

Addie heard hurried footsteps, then looked up to see Josh framed in the door of the stall.

With a startled exclamation, he hastened to her, kneeling at her side and crushing her to him, goo and all.

"I was so scared when I couldn't find you in the house. Are you okay?"

Addie nodded, not trusting her voice.

Pete appeared, rushing to Clementine and the foal. "What happened?" he asked gruffly.

"You have a beautiful new filly," she said weakly.

"Is she okay?" Josh called to Pete where he was checking Clementine.

"She's fine. But it looks like a red bag delivery. This little filly should be dead right now."

Both men looked at Addie.

"Well, I don't know the technical term for it," Addie explained. "The foal wasn't coming out first. I used the stool leg to cut the red bag. Then I broke the water and got the foal out."

Pete and Josh's mouths dropped open. Their lengthy, dumfounded stares made Addie want to squirm. Even when Clementine stood to her feet, the two men kept their eyes fixed on Addie.

"Addie, how did you know how to do that?" Josh asked in amazement.

Addie thought. "Well, I used to read a lot of dime novels—."

"You learned how to birth a horse in a dime novel?" Pete snorted incredulously.

"No," Addie said, shooting him a look of impatience. "When I was younger, some of the books I read had stuff about horses. I started asking our stable hand a lot of questions, and he finally let me sit in on some births. My dad wasn't happy about his daughter spending so much time in the stable, but I was lonely. I guess I learned quite a bit about horses."

Silence descended again, but this time, Addie thought she recognized something more than surprise in their gazes. They held a hint of respect.

Their study of Addie only ended when the filly struggled to her feet and stood on wobbly legs.

Pete stretched, apparently satisfied that the new foal was healthy. He turned to leave the stall, then paused and looked back at Josh and Addie. "Hey, Josh, do you think the mercantile will be open in the morning?"

"I don't see why not." Josh said, obviously taken aback by the strange question. "It's not a Sunday. Why do you ask?

Pete called over his shoulder as he walked out. "I'm thinkin' I need to get me some of them dime novels."

Chapter 10

"DERN fool man!"

Pete slammed the door with enough force to make the windows rattle as he stomped through the kitchen. Addie jumped, sloshing coffee all over the table.

"Who's the fool today, Pete?" she asked, tiredly wiping up the spill with a small hand towel. It was the morning after Clementine's foaling, and everyone was exhausted. Addie had stumbled into bed just a few hours before sunrise. Josh had told her to sleep in, that she had earned it, but she chose to rise shortly after Josh left, donning Charlotte's green gingham, freshly washed and dried in the sun after its bath in the river. She wanted to look her best today.

Despite numerous attempts to tell Josh the truth about who she was, someone or something had always arisen preventing her. She vowed that the next time she saw Josh, she would not let anyone or any unfortunate mishap stop her from telling him the truth. Addie just hoped he wouldn't hate her once he knew it.

"Hank, that's who!" Pete fumed, tossing his hat on the table before slouching in a chair. "He went and got himself hurt yesterday, which is why we were so late ridin' back to the ranch. Got kicked in the ribs by that mean ol' horse of Clint's. Insisted he was just bruised. Well, now this morning, he's laid up in bed and can't hardly breathe. Josh is on his way to go get the doc."

"Oh, no! That's horrible. Is there anything I can do to help?"

Pete eyed Addie warily. "I don't suppose you can manage making some grub for the ranch hands, can ya? Hank was supposed to be cooking up breakfast, but he can't raise a finger without yowling like a polecat."

Addie paused before answering. "I think I can make something." Surely she could figure out how to scramble some eggs?

"No bacon," Pete looked pointedly at her.

"I wouldn't dream of it," Addie said haughtily, her eyes flashing.

"How about biscuits and gravy? Seems like Josh mentioned that you knew how to bake a mean biscuit."

"Okay," Addie agreed hesitantly.

Pete rose from the table. "Cook it in here, and when you're done, I'll help you carry it to the bunkhouse. That's where the men eat. Make enough for a dozen."

Pete left Addie standing uncertainly in the kitchen. She didn't know how to make biscuits. What were the ingredients? Flour, and what else?

Tears pooled in her eyes. She thought last night marked a turning point. Josh and Pete had been so impressed with her care of Clementine and the filly. Now she would disappoint them again with her lack of cooking skills.

Addie searched the kitchen, hoping to find some type of recipe or instructions for making biscuits. But it was to no avail. She had to tell Pete she couldn't do it. Then she would wait for Josh to come back with the doctor. She must tell him the truth, hoping that he understood.

But she knew he wouldn't. Maybe it would be enough to convince Josh that Pete was right–women didn't belong on ranches.

Worse, all of the men would go hungry if she didn't come up with something for them to eat

Tears streamed down Addie's face.

Not knowing what else to do, she found a big bowl and put some flour in it. She added a little salt and a handful of sugar. Eggs. Weren't eggs usually used in something that was baked? She cracked one egg, being careful not to get any of the shell into the mixture.

That went so well, she wondered if she needed to add more. After all, she was baking for twelve people. Before she had time to second guess herself, she added five more eggs. Retrieving some fresh milk, she added a couple of cups of that as well. She stirred it all up, like Josh had showed her when making the cornbread.

With a spoon, she took a tiny bit out and tasted it. Addie made a face. Tasted salty and bland. She added in a handful more of sugar and some more milk. More stirring.

But the dough was way too wet. She lifted the spoon and let the mixture plop back into the bowl. This was hopeless! It resembled lumpy soup rather than biscuit dough!

Addie swiped at more tears with her sleeve, accidentally leaving a trail of dough across her cheek. She tried to wipe it away, but feared she'd just made it worse.

The only thing she could think to do was add more flour; maybe then it wouldn't be so wet. She reached into the flour sack with her jar. Scooping up a generous supply, she carefully brought it up to the bowl, right as a firm knock echoed at the front door.

Startled, Addie jerked, sending the flour up and raining all over her.

With a shaking hand, Addie set the almost empty jar on the counter and tried to dust herself off while she hurried to the front of the house.

Who could be at the door? Pete wouldn't knock, and the ranch hands would use the kitchen door.

Giving up on the white powder still decorating her dress, Addie hastily dried her eyes with the hem of her apron. With a deep breath, Addie opened the door, her welcoming smile dying on her lips.

A blonde with a gentle smile gazed back at her. A blonde wearing her white blouse and gold skirt.

Charlotte Mason had arrived.

"Why, hello, Miss Delaney," she said sweetly. "Or can I call you Adelaide? Or do you prefer something else? I feel like we are close friends after the mix up with our carpet bags. I'm so sorry about that. But see, I've brought it back to you safe and sound." Charlotte held out the carpet bag as if it was a peace offering.

Addie didn't know what to say. In the brief moments when she had allowed herself to wonder about Charlotte, she had always imagined her as being very angry at what Addie had done. But the serene woman standing before her didn't seem mad at all!

Woodenly, Addie accepted the carpet bag with a simple, "Thank you."

What should she do? Should she welcome her in? She needed to explain, to tell her what had happened and apologize, but she didn't know where to begin.

Charlotte, on the other hand, seemed not to share Addie's lack of words.

"Oh, good! You're wearing my dress! That means you must also have my trunk. I was afraid you might have only two dresses to wear, your travel suit and the spare in my bag. I took the liberty of claiming your trunk as well, hoping I'd be able to find you and return it. We have it in the back of the wagon. I hope you don't mind, but I've worn your clothes too." Charlotte looked at Addie and sighed with contentment. "I guess the Lord knew what he was doing when we met up in St. Louis and had our bags switched. Imagine how difficult it would have been if we would have been different sizes! Although, I don't blame the Good Lord for my own foolishness in grabbing the wrong bag. Thankfully, we know that everything happens for a reason, right?"

Addie had forgotten about Charlotte Mason's monologues. Addie stood, staring, for the entirety of Charlotte's rambling, her mind not able to move past the shock of Charlotte being here at the Bar H.

Suddenly, panic hit. Addie needed to find Josh. She must talk to him before he met the "real Charlotte."

"Nice to see you again, Miss Delaney."

Another person stood on the porch. Addie's eyes swerved from Charlotte to the man beside her. In her shock of seeing Charlotte, she had completely missed the other visitor. Blake Trenton, her fiancé, stood in all his formal glory, exactly as Addie remembered him.

Dressed in a freshly pressed suit and taking advantage of every inch of his towering height, his somber brown eyes assessed Addie. "You are looking well. Your father will be relieved to know that no harm has befallen you on your little adventure."

"Y-yes, I'm quite well. Thank you."

Just then, Clint stepped up to the porch, his hat in his hands.

"Hi, Miss Addie. Sorry to interrupt. Pete sent me to see if you needed any help making breakfast for the ranch hands."

Breakfast! At the sight of Charlotte, she had completely forgotten her task.

Now she just wanted to fold down right there on the porch, bury her face in her hands, and cry. First breakfast and now Charlotte and Blake! She couldn't take anymore!

"I'm sorry, Clint," she said breathlessly, trying to speak past the little breath hiccups that warned of coming sobs. "I will talk to Pete. I don't know that I can make it today."

"I can help!" Charlotte said quickly, enthusiastically bobbing her head, her fine blonde hair blowing with the movement. "Just point me to the kitchen. We will have breakfast ready in no time."

"Wonderful! I'll go tell Pete you ladies have it under control."

Clint hurried down the steps, seemingly relieved to be given a reprieve from kitchen duty.

Charlotte turned to the man beside her. "Blake, I mean, Mr. Trenton, would you like to wait in the parlor while I help Addie?"

At his formal nod, Charlotte stepped past Addie into the house, spinning in a circle, a happy smile on her angelic face. "The house is beautiful! It's exactly how I imagined it would be when Joshua described it in his letters. This place already feels like home."

A lump rose in Addie's throat. The Bar H felt like Addie's home as well. Actually, where Josh was felt like home.

"Is the kitchen through here?" Charlotte questioned.

Addie nodded, not trusting herself to speak.

"Oh, and here is the parlor. Please make yourself comfortable, Mr. Trenton. Would you like a cup of coffee or tea?" Charlotte was already stepping into her role as mistress of the house.

"I'm fine, thank you, Miss Mason," Blake said. He stood at the door to the parlor, "Miss Delaney, I look forward to speaking to you after your… duties… are complete."

Addie walked woodenly behind Charlotte, dreading that conversation.

"Do you have a spare apron? I would hate to ruin these lovely clothes of yours that I am wearing. I suppose I could go change into one of my own dresses. Although I think we are in a bit of a hurry this morning, am I correct?"

Addie nodded again.

"What are we making for breakfast?" Charlotte asked, taking a metal bowl off of a shelf.

"Biscuits and gravy."

"Oh, perfect! I will get started on the biscuits. Do you want to make the gravy?"

"I don't know how," Addie said quietly.

"Oh, no trouble. You just tell me where I can find things, and I will take care of everything."

Addie watched Charlotte as she lit the wood stove. With an occasional question, she quickly located all her ingredients and began assembling breakfast.

Addie saw the instant Charlotte spotted the bowl of goo that Addie had tried to make. Pausing the work with her own bowl, Charlotte stuck her finger delicately into the mixture, then tasted it. Addie waited for Charlotte's cry of disgust and reprimand, but it never came. Instead, she quickly added a few ingredients Addie didn't recognize, and then poured a portion into a circle on a hot pan.

"Do you think the men will mind a few flapjacks to go with their biscuits and gravy?" Charlotte asked. "This mixture is going to make some wonderful flapjacks!"

"I'm sure they won't mind at all," Addie said numbly. Charlotte could even make something wonderful out of Addie's mess!

Addie worked to fight off the tears. This was the wife Josh deserved, the help-mate he needed. Charlotte belonged at the Bar H, not Addie.

Within minutes, Charlotte had the gravy simmering on the stove, biscuits lining a pan, ready to be placed into the oven, and a steadily increasing stack of golden flapjacks. Charlotte made it all look so easy.

Addie knew differently.

"There we go," Charlotte said, closing the door on the oven. "Those will bake up in just a few, and we will be ready. So tell me, Addie, are you upset with me about the bag switch?"

Addie shook her head, tears beginning to fall.

"There, there. Why are you crying? I'm so sorry. I feel terrible about taking your bag and ticket when you needed them. Has it been really rough?"

"No, really. I'm fine. Josh has been wonderful."

"Joshua?" Charlotte's brows rose. "What's he like? Is he here? I didn't see him when we drove in. Of course, I've only ever seen his picture."

Ah... yes, the picture that had started this all. "He went to get the doctor. Hank, the cook, is hurt. He should be back shortly,"

Addie planned on speaking to Josh privately as soon as he rode in. Should Addie tell Charlotte that she was married to Josh? *Was* Addie married to Josh? She certainly hoped so. While she had been attracted to Josh's handsome face in his picture, and when they met, she had grown to care about him deeply over their few short days together. His ready smile and teasing ways were a wonderful change from the environment Addie was accustomed to in New York with her father.

"What happened to you in St. Louis, Charlotte?" Addie

asked, suddenly very curious about what had transpired. Had it been less than a week since that fateful afternoon? "I knew I had your carpetbag by mistake. I waited for you at your train, but you never arrived. Where did you go?"

A slight blush pinked Charlotte's cheeks, though Addie couldn't tell if it was from working over a hot stove, or embarrassment. She shot a hesitant glance in the direction of the parlor, as if afraid Blake might overhear her.

Finally, she simply replied, "I was indisposed."

Addie waited, expecting Charlotte to elaborate. But once again, when Addie *wanted* to hear Charlotte speak, she was silent. Which reminded Addie of the conversation they never finished in St. Louis, because Charlotte became 'indisposed.'

"Do you remember what we were discussing before you left?" Addie asked, inspecting her own hands. Strange how rough they felt after only a few days on the ranch. Stranger still that she didn't mind at all.

"Yes, I believe so," Charlotte replied, setting some butter and jelly on the table.

"I asked you a question about God's will," Addie reminded her. "How did you know God's will for your life?"

Charlotte brought two warm mugs filled with the coffee she had just made, and set one before Addie. Taking a seat as well, Charlotte turned to Addie, her normally jovial expression, surprisingly serious.

"You want to know how I determined that it was God's will for me to be a mail order bride?"

Addie nodded.

"Let me start with a question for you? Have you ever felt

a strong urging to do something, even though it didn't necessarily make sense?"

Addie thought, remembering not being able to sleep last night. She had repeatedly felt a strong conviction that she should check on Clementine, even though it didn't made sense. If she hadn't heeded that urging, Clementine's foal would have died. Had that been God speaking to her?

Addie slowly nodded, answering Charlotte's question while pondering what it all meant.

Charlotte sipped her coffee, musing aloud, "Sometimes God's voice is like that, telling us the right thing to do, but sometimes it isn't. God's voice is always in his Word, the Bible, but sometimes we don't get that extra help to tell us which direction to take."

"What about you?" Addie asked, afraid Charlotte might leave her answers vague. "Did God give you an inclination that you couldn't ignore?"

"Not exactly," Charlotte clarified. "After my mother died, I earnestly prayed and searched the Bible for guidance. I didn't know what to do, now that I was alone without any family. I bought a newspaper one morning, looking for jobs as a cook or governess. Instead, I saw Joshua's advertisement. I was intrigued by the idea of becoming a mail order bride. After all, I enjoy cooking, but my dream has always been to marry and have a family of my own. This would fulfill both of my desires. I continued to pray and sought godly counsel from the reverend at the church I attended. I don't know how to fully explain it, but I felt a sense of peace about my decision."

Charlotte paused, searching Addie's face imploringly. "Sometimes God speaks directly to you, but other times you just have to knock on a lot of doors and see which one He opens. I saw Joshua's advertisement in the newspaper, and I felt the Lord tell me, not in words but in my spirit, that I should be a mail order bride. The sense of peace about my decision has never wavered, even after I missed my train and had to go to Denver with your ticket."

Addie took a deep breath. "Charlotte, there's something I have to tell you. I'm really sorry about taking your ticket and your place here at the ranch. I waited for you at the station in St. Louis, but when you didn't come, I didn't know what to do. I had no ticket, and I held yours in my hand. So I used it. Then one thing led to another."

Addie moaned and closed her eyes. "I never intended for any of this to happen!"

"Oh, Addie, it isn't your fault!" Charlotte assured, grasping one of Addie's hands in hers, trying to offer comfort. "I don't blame you at all! I'm the one who grabbed the wrong bag. Don't feel bad! Besides, it doesn't matter now. We can trade bags and places. You'll go back with Mr. Trenton, and I'll stay here with my Joshua. It doesn't matter how we got here, the important thing is that everything is exactly as it should be!"

"But it isn't!" Addie protested, tears once again stinging her eyes. "That's what I'm trying to explain. It's all very much my fault! I didn't just take your belongings, I took—"

"It smells mighty fine in here!" Pete announced, appearing through the back door. "If that grub is ready, I'll help you feed those hungry rascals down at the bunkhouse."

Leaving Addie, Charlotte bustled over to the oven and opened it.

"All ready!" she announced triumphantly, pulling out the

pan of lightly golden biscuits. Having made a double batch, Charlotte replaced the pan in the oven with another, so that the men would have plenty.

Her confession on hold, Addie stood to help carry the food. Charlotte emptied the biscuits into a basket and handed it to Addie, while she carried the pot of gravy and assigned Pete the plate of pancakes.

Pete led the parade down to the bunkhouse. Having never been there, Addie entered hesitantly. The men already sat at a long table bordered by benches on either side. Though she had met a few of them, like Clint, there were other faces she didn't recognize.

Feeling uncomfortable, she hurriedly set her offering on the table and attempted to retreat, only to run smack into the solid chest of Josh.

Josh caught her. "It looks like you've been busy, Addie," he said with a proud smile.

"Oh, it wasn't me. I didn't... I... I..." Once again, Addie was reduced to a stuttering mess.

Resolutely, she lifted her chin and looked her husband squarely in the eye. "Josh, could I speak with you outside?"

"Oh, Addie!" Charlotte gushed brightly. "Is this Joshua?"

"Mrs. Harding?" A voice boomed from the crowded table.

Everyone turned.

One of the ranch hands addressed Addie, a big grin stretching his worn face. "Ma'am, these are the best biscuits and gravy I ever done ate!"

Numerous other men, their mouths full, grunted and

exclaimed in agreement.

Another man managed to call out to Josh, "Boss, looks like you got yourself a keeper!"

"Mrs. Harding?" Charlotte repeated, turning to Addie.

Addie watched the confusion vanish in Charlotte's eyes, anger quickly sparking and taking its place. Watching the transformation in Charlotte's blue depths, Addie was both fascinated and strangely terrified. Apparently, the angelic woman was capable of having a temper. And Addie knew she was about to feel the full effect of it. Worse, she knew she deserved everything Charlotte gave her.

"Addie, who is this?" she heard Josh ask.

But her eyes were locked with Charlotte, and she made no attempt to hide the miserable truth and guilt she knew lay in her own.

"Adelaide Delaney, you married my *husband?*" Charlotte accused, incredulous.

"Well, he wasn't your husband at the time!" Addie weakly defended.

"Addie who is this?" Josh asked again, this time demanding.

Finally, feeling like she'd lost everything she could ever value in life, Addie choked out the truth. "Joshua Harding, let me introduce Charlotte Mason, *your wife.*"

And then, Addie ran.

Chapter 11

ADDIE stumbled down the rutted path, a sharp, stabbing pain in her lungs forcing her desperate flight to a walk. She clutched her aching side, the physical discomfort no match for the agony that pierced her heart. Tears streamed unchecked down her face, rivers through the dust and flour that coated it. She had fled from the bunkhouse with no destination in mind other than away.

Now she stood on a wagon-rutted path. She didn't know where she was going, but hopefully it was toward Last Chance and the train that would carry her away from the consequences of her actions.

The air was warm, the Texas sun beating down steadily from near directly overhead. Addie had lost track of how long she'd been walking, but with the angle of the sun and soreness of her feet, it sure seemed like hours. Addie put her hand to her sweat-beaded forehead, looking in the distance to catch some glimpse of the town, but all she saw was open land. She hoped to make it to Last Chance in time to catch a train, but with no end in sight, and no possible rescue, discouragement settled in to blend with her heartbreak.

She had lost Josh, that much was certain. Though he was not really hers to begin with. He was Charlotte's, and Addie had stolen what was not hers to take. Now she was suffering the consequences, as she rightfully should.

Addie regretted her actions immensely. She should have been honest with Josh from the moment she had stepped off of the train. Oh, she had tried numerous times to speak the truth, but she should have persisted and not married Josh under false pretenses. Now she was left with a broken heart and the guilt of knowing she'd hurt people she cared about.

Addie loved Josh. And Charlotte had shown her nothing but kindness when they met in St. Louis and when she arrived at the Bar H. Neither of these people deserved the deceit that Addie had dealt them. Addie was a Christian, but she hadn't been living like one.

Addie's feet felt heavy as she took one step, and then another. Gradually her shuffling steps slowed until she felt she couldn't lift her pointed boot one more step down the dirt road.

She stopped, lifting her eyes to the blue sky above. "Lord, forgive me," she choked out. "I was wrong to deceive and hide the truth. Help Josh and Charlotte with the hurt I've caused them, and if possible, help me atone for what I've done."

Addie held still, waiting for peace or any assurance that her desperate prayer had been heard. But the whisper of a breeze was the only response.

A rumble from behind startled Addie out of her vigil. A wagon approached.

Addie quickly resumed walking, her head bent, refusing to turn and look at the driver.

"Can I offer you a ride, Miss Delaney, or should I say, Mrs. Harding?"

Addie stopped mid-stride, turning to face the wagon. Blake Trenton's blonde hair shone brightly in the sun, his hands gripping leather reins loosely.

"You know?" Addie asked, embarrassment once again creeping into her already flushed cheeks.

Blake nodded. "I got directions to the Bar H from a man who worked at the livery where I rented this wagon. His name was George, and he said he had recently served as a witness for the wedding of the owner of the Bar H, Josh Harding, and his mail order bride. Since Miss Mason was with me, I naturally assumed you were the bride to whom he referred."

"But you didn't tell Charlotte," Addie was sure that Charlotte's surprise had been genuine. She had not known that Josh and Addie were married.

"I did not share what I was told with Miss Mason. I thought it best to speak to you first. Besides, I didn't want to make any rash judgements based on the account of George, the liveryman."

"Thank you. That was very generous of you."

Blake brushed off her thanks with a wave of his hand. "Where are you headed now?"

"I don't know. The train depot? I can't stay here

anymore."

"Please let me offer my assistance. I will drive you wherever you want to go," Blake said, offering his hand to help her into the wagon.

Addie hesitated, but reluctantly accepted Blake's hand. Blake was another person she had wronged. She had so many apologies to make. This one she could administer in person, the others, to Charlotte and Josh, would have to be made in a letter.

"Mr. Trenton," Addie began, once she settled on the seat. Having learned her lesson the hard way, she was not willing to wait for a more appropriate time to do what was right. "I am very sorry for not arriving in Denver as planned. I know our fathers had a business merger that hinged upon our marriage. I acted foolishly and caused a lot of pain to many people. But I am prepared to suffer the consequences of my recent actions."

Blake spoke carefully, his eyes on the road. "Miss Mason led me to believe that the fault for your switched places was entirely her own. As for the business deal between our fathers, that will continue regardless of our engagement being terminated."

"You won't marry me now?" Not that she blamed him, but having been lectured by her father on the importance of her marriage, she was surprised by Blake's calmly-spoken words.

"I don't make a habit of marrying another man's wife, Mrs. Harding."

Addie looked at her hands clasped in front of her. "We weren't technically married," Addie said wistfully. "The reverend did not use my name when administering the vows." Not wanting Blake to think the worst of her, she added, blushing, "Josh was very much a gentleman, and we didn't have a marriage, but in name. And that name was the wrong one. Josh married Charlotte Mason. Not Adelaide Delaney."

His voice still unperturbed, Blake spoke thoughtfully, "I believe Shakespeare wrote, 'a rose by any other name would smell as sweet.' But more importantly, I believe that in the eyes of God, you and Mr. Harding are married. Which is why our engagement is null and void."

Addie couldn't make herself feel sorry for this outcome. She had not wanted to marry Blake, nor he her. Had they not been forced by their fathers, perhaps they could have been friends on their own. Blake was certainly showing her kindness now, kindness she in no way deserved.

"Thank you for not canceling the business deal," she said sincerely. "I'm sure my father will appreciate you upholding your side of the transaction, when I did not."

"He already knows," Blake stated, nodding firmly. "I informed him of the mix-up when Miss Mason arrived and you did not. I severed our engagement prior to my arrival with Miss Mason to Texas. Had you not been already married, I still would not marry you. I never believed we were a good match. I simply agreed to the arrangement for the sake of my family's business. However, I've come to realize that I cannot marry a woman I do not love, not for any reason." Blake paused. "Your father has requested that I place you on a train for New York immediately."

Addie shivered despite the rising heat of the day. She was grateful that her father would not lose his lucrative partnership, but he would be furious when he learned of Addie's behavior. Her father would punish her severely for what happened. There was no doubt.

She had lived with a man as his wife, even though it was in name only. Texas was a long way from New York, but she had no desire to marry another man. Hopefully her father would see her as 'ruined' and not force her into another marriage.

"Do you want me to purchase a train ticket for you?" Blake asked.

They were nearing Last Chance now. Addie could see the outlines of the buildings.

"Yes. I think that would be for the best," Addie answered quietly.

"We don't have to leave on the train today. Perhaps you should speak with Mr. Harding before you leave." Blake suggested. "He seemed very upset by your departure."

Addie's head snapped up. "You spoke with Josh?"

"Only momentarily. The ranch was in quite the uproar. Miss Mason introduced me as your fiancé. That seemed to only add to the fervor."

Addie hung her head in shame.

"If it's any consolation, Mr. Harding was extremely upset, so much so that he would have hit me square in the jaw had I not ducked. I assured Mr. Harding that you and I were no longer engaged. Miss Mason pointed me in the right direction, and I made a hasty departure to find you."

"Josh tried to punch you?" Addie asked incredulously.

"He would have succeeded eventually if a man, I believe it was his uncle, hadn't restrained him," Blake said wryly.

They came to a stop in front of the train depot. Addie's

eyes settled on the spot where she and Josh had spoken their vows only a few days prior.

"Will you be leaving with me?" Addie asked quietly, lost in her memories.

"Yes, I have a personal matter to attend to. I will ride with you as far as I am permitted before taking a train to Denver," Blake jumped down from the wagon. "Why don't you freshen up before we depart? By the looks of it, we don't have much time before the train will be leaving. The workers are already loading up the trunks."

Addie really didn't care what she looked like right now, but Blake had been very kind to her. She didn't want to embarrass him any further with her ragged appearance. She splashed water on her face in the small powder room of the depot, removing the traces of her failed attempts at making biscuits. Finishing quickly, she waited on the platform for Blake.

After several minutes, he appeared and spoke to the porters about securing her trunk and his luggage. Addie's carpet bag had been left at the ranch. Addie was relieved. She never wanted to lay eyes on a brown floral carpet bag again.

"All ready," Blake said, joining her on the platform. "The conductor says we can board now. We are the last passengers."

Blake helped Addie up the steps of the train. He seemed to sense that she was in danger of falling apart any minute. He found seats for them, positioning himself at the window, so she would not have to see out.

Addie was grateful. She was having difficulty swallowing past the lump in her throat. And despite her resolve to not embarrass Blake, tears soon trailed down her cheeks.

A satin handkerchief gently pressed into her hand.

"Thank you," Addie said, dabbing at the tears that showed no sign of slowing. "I'm sorry. I can't seem to stop."

"It's alright, Adelaide." It was the first time Blake had ever used her first name.

"Are you sure you want to leave? We can wait if that would make you feel better. You really should speak to Mr. Harding before you leave."

Addie shook her head. "I know I'm a coward, but I can't face him."

Blake studied her, nodded once, and faced the window, leaving her to cry privately.

The train whistle blew, signaling departure. A few seconds later, the whistle blew again.

But the train didn't move.

After several minutes of waiting, the train remained still, and the whispering began.

"What's happening?"

"Why aren't we moving?"

Addie heard several passengers anxiously asking questions, while others appeared to be getting angry. When there was no response and the train still sat, some even leaned out the windows.

"Some cowboy on a horse is is standing on the tracks!" someone gasped.

"What is he doing?"

More passengers clambered to the windows.

Addie looked to Blake in confusion. "What's happening?"

Blake stood and joined the others with his head leaning out a window.

To Addie's surprise, he quickly sat back down without saying a word, a smile creasing his normally somber look.

Addie opened her mouth to question him again, but she was interrupted by a disgruntled gentleman with a handlebar mustache.

"This is ridiculous! Someone call the sheriff!"

Another passenger, who was talking out the window to someone on the ground outside, turned back around and reported. "He's just standing there saying something about needing a 'fool woman on a ranch.'"

"Addie!"

Addie's body jerked in surprise. Her heart clenched once before it started pounding. She recognized that voice!

"I didn't think he would let you go so easily," Blake said, his face now wreathed in a full smile. "Mrs. Harding, I believe your husband has come to collect you."

"Sir, this is highly irregular. I cannot permit you to board this train." Despite his words to the contrary, the conductor slowly backed down the aisle, moving aside so that Josh could pass. "We have a schedule to keep."

"I will just be a moment. I need to speak with my wife."

Addie thrilled at his words. He still considered them married!

Josh's eyes were dangerously dark, shooting blue flames, especially when they rested on Addie and who sat next to her.

Addie rose slowly. "I'm so sorry, Josh. I never meant for this to happen. I tried so many times to tell you the truth."

"Where are you going?" Josh asked harshly, completely ignoring her apology. "Are you leaving with him?"

"N-nno," Addie stuttered. "Not really. I'm going back to New York. Mr. Trenton will be returning to Denver."

"Then I will be going with you."

"What?" Addie couldn't believe her ears.

"You are my wife, where you go, I will go. If you say you are going to New York, I will be the one sitting beside you on the train that takes you there." Josh shot a glare at Blake.

Blake held up his hands as if in surrender. "More than happy to move."

"Josh," Addie said quietly, mindful of the raised eyebrows and whispers from the other passengers on the train. "We aren't married, not really. Reverend Gates used Charlotte's name in our vows."

"A fact that I intend to remedy immediately. Perdition is a stop on the way. That's where Reverend Gates said he was headed to solve the potluck dispute."

"You don't even know my real name," Addie whispered.

"Yes, I do. Addie Harding," Josh placed a finger beneath her chin, gently lifting so that he could look directly into her eyes. "You are my wife. That doesn't change just because your name did. I married you. Not your name."

Addie couldn't believe what was happening. But a dark cloud hung over her happiness. Charlotte. Addie couldn't hurt her again.

"What about Charlotte? What will she do now? She has no family. I've ruined all of her plans."

"Charlotte was upset at first, but I think she was mostly surprised. She recovered quickly and was very worried about you. We talked on the way into town to look for you. She wanted me to tell you that your bags were switched for a reason. Sometimes God opens a door for you, and sometimes he leaves you a ticket in a carpet bag. God works all things together for good. He has other plans for Charlotte Mason from Georgia."

Addie nodded. She wouldn't have thought it possible to receive a pardon, but she already knew what a forgiving, selfless person Charlotte was. She couldn't help but still feel like Josh deserved better than Adelaide Delaney.

"Josh, I am so sorry I deceived you. I want to be your wife more than anything else, but you deserve more than me. You are a rancher. You need a wife who can cook and not cause a disaster every other minute!"

"I need you," Josh said firmly. "God brought us together, Addie Harding. I don't doubt that. Now you don't either."

"But you don't know me. You know Charlotte. You wrote to her, not me."

"You don't think I know you?" Josh grinned. "I know you are afraid of mice, but you are not afraid of delivering a horse. I know that you can't be trusted around a wood stove. I also know that I would rather eat burnt bacon for the rest of my life with you as my wife, than have the best biscuits in the world made by another woman."

Addie smiled tearfully, but Josh wasn't done. "And I know that I love you, Addie Harding, and I always will. I want you."

Completely overcome, she wrapped her arms around her husband and lifted her lips to meet his, not caring who watched. For at last, she was convinced that Josh Harding didn't want a Charlotte, he wanted an Addie.

Chapter 12

"OH, good! You're up," Charlotte exclaimed, entering the kitchen. "We need to hurry."

"Charlotte, it's barely dawn! Josh isn't even up yet!" Addie objected. The coffee wasn't hot yet, and she desperately needed coffee. After hearing Charlotte's feet on the stairs, she had managed to drag herself out of bed, but barely.

"We have a lot to do today," Charlotte explained as she bustled around pulling ingredients down from the cupboards. "Pete told me to have you check on that little filly. What did you name her? Georgia? Anyway, he said he thinks she may have a scratch on her leg and wants your opinion."

A flush of pleasure washed over Addie's face. Pete wanted her opinion, and more than that, she suspected he may have made an exception for her in his feelings about women and ranches.

After pouring herself a mug of coffee, Charlotte turned back to Addie. "Do you think you can check on her after breakfast? With your father coming for the noon meal, I need to start preparing for that while you get breakfast for Josh and Pete."

Addie's face must have given away the panic she felt.

Charlotte rushed to reassure her. "You can do it, Addie. I've shown you how, and you've done a wonderful job of helping all week. It's time you tried yourself. Don't worry, you won't be alone. I'll be right here if you have a problem or need any help."

Addie took a deep breath and reluctantly nodded. She could do this.

"Thank you, Charlotte," she said earnestly.

"For what? I haven't done anything yet."

"Yes, you have. For starters, you forgave me for stealing your intended, even though I didn't deserve forgiveness. Then, at the last minute, you came with us on the train to Perdition to be a witness for our wedding. Then you agreed to stay here and teach me to cook, clean, and everything else that goes along with being a rancher's wife. You are such a good teacher, and so patient. I don't know what I'd do without you. I'm just so thankful to God that you stayed even after the way I treated you."

Charlotte smiled, reaching out to impulsively hug her friend. "Like I said before, everything turned out the way it should, though God sure had a funny way of getting us here! You and Josh love each other, and I couldn't stand in the way of what God put together. As far as me staying, you're paying me well. And I like being here with you, at least for the time being. But remember, this is only a temporary arrangement. I still have my own plans. I have to follow God's will for me."

"I know," Addie assured, trying not to be fear-stricken at the thought of Charlotte leaving.

Addie was so thankful she and Charlotte had gotten to talk after the newly remarried Hardings had returned on the train. Though the other woman had accepted the job at the ranch, she made it clear that she would not be staying for any great length of time.

"I'm just thankful for each day I have you," Addie said sincerely. "You've already taught me so much."

"And now it's time to test those skills," Charlotte said briskly. "You mix up the biscuits and get started on some bacon and eggs while I pluck the chicken. Then we'll make pies, maybe some dinner rolls, and vegetables. I picked a mess of green beans yesterday. I'll show you how to snap them."

"The chicken?" Addie asked, ignoring the rest of Charlotte's chatter to focus on the one word that filled her with instant dread.

"Yes, I thought fried chicken would be a good meal to have with your father. I'll get the bird ready and then show you how to make my prizewinning recipe."

"So, you already killed the chicken?"

"Yes, I should have waited to give you a lesson in killing chickens, but I wanted to get it done early. I don't want your father to have to wait to eat, so we need to focus on pies and actually frying the chicken. I'm sure we'll have another opportunity for you to kill a chicken soon."

"Which chicken did you kill?" Addie demanded, her voice shaking. "Tell me it wasn't Patrick Henry!"

At Charlotte's bewildered face, Addie urgently tried again. "Did you kill a rooster?"

"No," Charlotte replied, as if it was an absurd idea.

Instant relief flooded through Addie. Patrick Henry was safe. And if she didn't kill a rooster, that meant Paul Revere was safe too. But the hens…

"Which hen did you kill?" Addie demanded.

"Addie, I have no idea what you're talking about. I didn't ask the chicken's name before I chopped off its head!"

Addie winced. "Please tell me it wasn't Martha Washington or Abigail Adams. Those two are my favorites."

Obviously baffled, Charlotte sighed, shaking her head. "It was one of the younger ones, Addie. She walked kind of funny, so I thought she was a good candidate."

"Oh," Addie said, recognizing the chicken from Charlotte's description. "I hadn't named her yet."

Charlotte brightened. "See? That's good! Now I will show you how to make a delicious dinner out of the nameless chicken, and you won't have to feel bad at all. What kind of pie do you think goes best with fried chicken? I think I saw some berries, but I'm rather partial to apple. Maybe I'll look to see if Josh has some apples. I know it's not quite apple season, but sometimes even canned or dried fruit can make a wonderful pie. What do you think?

But Addie hadn't been paying attention. Instead, she

stared unseeing out the window.

"Addie?" Charlotte questioned.

"Oh, sorry." Addie snapped out of her reverie. "Can we decide about the pie after breakfast? I just don't think I can think about more than one meal at a time. I'll get started on the bacon and biscuits, and then you can check on me after you're done plucking Joan."

"Joan?" Charlotte's normally smooth brow scrunched in confusion. "Who's Joan."

"Joan of Arc. The chicken."

Charlotte paused, her mouth dropping open. "Addie Harding, you can't do that! You can't name a chicken after it's dead!"

Addie shrugged, ignoring Charlotte, and measuring flour into the bowl.

Her confusion now progressing to amusement, Charlotte laughed at her friend. Shaking her head, Charlotte left Addie to her biscuits and retreated outside.

Addie was not fast, but she carefully mixed up a double batch of biscuits and cut them out. She made sure the oven was lit and stocked appropriately, then slid them in to bake.

Next, she decided that she would do the bacon before the eggs. There was no way she was confident enough to do both at the same time.

Her heart fluttered as she lay the bacon into the pan, memories of her previous attempt making her nervous. She vowed to stand right in front of the oven and turn the bacon every twenty seconds. There would be no repeat disaster!

Five minutes into her bacon task, she'd turned the strips

so often they were barely warm.

Suddenly, she felt strong arms reach around from behind and pull her back. Josh nuzzled her neck, and she couldn't resist turning to meet her lips with his.

"Why didn't you stay in bed longer?" Josh whispered huskily. "I missed you. I don't like waking up and finding you gone."

"I wanted to stay, but Charlotte has a long list of things for us to do before my father arrives."

"And how are you feeling about your pa's visit?"

"I think it will be fine. I'm married. He got his business deal. There's not really anything he can do about it. I'm glad we decided to not go to New York right after traveling to Perdition to have Reverend Gates renew our vows. Blake Trenton was kind enough to hand deliver my letter when my father arrived in Denver. The telegram Father sent us in reply sounded friendly enough. He said congratulations and asked if he could give his well-wishes in person. That doesn't really sound like he's angry, so I'm really not anxious about his visit. I think the fact that my husband owns one of the largest cattle ranches in Texas doesn't hurt!"

Satisfied with her answer, Josh brushed the stray hairs from her face and once again began nuzzling her neck.

Addie frowned, "The only thing I'm worried about is the cooking. Charlotte is plucking Joan, and I'm supposed to be making—the bacon!"

She tried to turn back, but Josh held her, placing kisses that tickled up toward her mouth.

"Josh, let me go! The bacon is going to burn!"

"That's the way I like it, remember?"

Addie laughed and surrendered. She knew she was very weak when faced with the temptation of her husband's kisses.

The screech of the screen door was followed by a gasp. "Addie what are you doing? The bacon is burning!"

Addie broke away from Josh as Charlotte ran to rescue the rapidly browning meat.

"I'm sorry, Charlotte, I was just…"

Her eyes swung back to Josh, seeking help, but Josh remained mute, simply lifting his eyebrows as if curious what kind of excuse she was going to up with.

But she was drawing a complete blank.

At Addie's pause, Charlotte filled in, her tone teasingly naïve. "Oh, did Josh have something on his face?"

At her friend's suggestion, a sly grin lifted the corners of Addie's mouth, and she looked innocently up at her husband.

"Yes. Yes, he did. It was not an ant."

THE END

ENJOY this sneak peek at, ***Bride by Request***, book 2 in the ***Brides by Mail*** series coming soon.

St. Louis, Missouri, 1880

"Finally!" Charlotte Mason thought. With a nod and a smile to the woman exiting the small wooden structure, it was Charlotte's turn in the outhouse. There had been a long line of women waiting to use the facilities, longer than Charlotte had anticipated. Her train would leave shortly, but she had hoped to return in enough time to finish the conversation with the woman who had shared a bench with her while waiting for their trains.

Charlotte balanced her brown floral carpet bag in the crook of her arm, while she opened the wooden door with the other.

"Well, this certainly is one of the smaller outhouses I have ever had the displeasure to visit," Charlotte said dryly. She barely had any room to turn around.

She would have to mind the hem of her dress. She only had one other dress in her bag, and she had no idea how a person could possibly change clothing in a space the size of a postage stamp. Thankfully, the outhouse boasted a small corner shelf, just wide enough for her carpet bag, so at least her bag and its few possessions would be safe.

Shutting the door to the outhouse firmly behind her, Charlotte quickly turned to settle her bag onto the shelf.

Rrrriiippp!

Charlotte froze. She didn't breathe. She didn't move an inch.

Slowly closing her eyes, she whispered, "Please, please, please... Lord, do not let happen what I think just happened."

With unsteady hands, Charlotte reached for the fabric at the small of her back. Instead of feeling the poofed flounces of her bustle, she felt the thin fabric of her undergarments.

"Oh, no, no, no. This can't be happening!" Charlotte moaned, twisting at the waist to inspect the damage. Charlotte had seen drawings of the animals in Africa, and she was fairly certain that, with her brown dress and white cotton drawers showing her rump in the most improper way, she looked exactly like a baboon!

She could not leave the outhouse like this with her backside on full display for all the world to see! And she could hardly walk about with one hand clutching her bustle to her bottom all the way to Texas!

She lifted the worn brown fabric of her dress, trying to determine her best course of action. Her bustle was almost completely severed, hanging from her like a brown blob. Perhaps she could pin it in some way? Charlotte didn't think she had packed enough pins for this type of procedure. And the silver pins would definitely show. How humiliating!

A tentative knock followed by a woman's voice, had Charlotte quickly latching the outhouse door. "Is everything alright, in there, Miss? You've been in there quite a while. And there is a line forming."

"Be out in a minute!" Charlotte called with false cheerfulness. What was she going to do? There were multiple outhouses, but each had a long queue forming outside. Those expecting to use this outhouse were going to lose their patience very quickly.

Charlotte had packed a sewing kit in her carpet bag. It might take some extreme body contortions, but perhaps she could place a few quick stitches to attach her bustle back to her dress.

Yes, that is what she would do.

Feeling relieved that she had a plan, Charlotte opened the carpet bag.

"This isn't my bag," she whispered, dumbfounded. How did this happen?

The outhouse was rather dim, the only light filtering through the crescent moon shape at the top. Charlotte hadn't taken the time to study the bag in her haste to complete her toilette before her train left. Now, upon closer inspection, she realized that this carpet bag was far superior to her own. The pattern was more vibrant, and the little leather handles were stiff from being new. Charlotte's bag was worn from years of use while this one was obviously on its maiden voyage. And this carpet bag was vastly more expensive than her own. The feel of the fabric was thick and substantial, whereas hers was paper thin. This carpet bag must belong to a very wealthy woman.

Immediately Charlotte's mind flashed to her bench mate. The blonde haired woman was stylishly dressed. This must be her bag. After the woman had accidentally hit herself in the nose, Charlotte remembered stowing the woman's carpet bag next to her own under the bench.

A harsh pounding at the door startled Charlotte.

"Anybody in there?"

"Yes!" Charlotte replied meekly. "I will be out in a moment."

"There's a line here, Miss! The trains are leaving, and others need to get in there as well!"

"Out in a moment!" Charlotte could think of nothing else to say. She needed HER carpet bag if she was going to get out of this mess and still make her train.

Time for Plan B. Charlotte opened the outhouse door ever so slightly. Just enough that one eye was exposed. Two women stood waiting, their expressions hopeful when they saw Charlotte. Thankfully the rude man must have given up or used the other outhouse next to the one Charlotte occupied.

"Are you done, Miss?" The woman in front moved forward. She was short and plump with cheery red cheeks. She looked kindly enough. Perhaps this woman would help her. The second woman glowered sourly at Charlotte. Definitely not asking that one for help.

"Not quite," Charlotte said regretfully. "Can you please do me a small favor? I seem to have found myself in sort of an awkward predicament. I am in need of my carpet bag, and apparently, it was mistakenly switched with another woman's. Could you please be a dear and go to the platform closest to the train departing for Texas? There should be a woman waiting there on a bench. She is wearing a navy traveling suit, she has blonde hair, and a jaunty little hat. She has my carpet bag. Can you ask her to bring it to me? I am desperately in need of it."

A light of understanding dawned on the woman's face while Charlotte explained her needs. The woman was nodding her head vigorously before Charlotte was even done talking.

Bless her! Charlotte thought as the little woman hurried off to complete her errand.

Charlotte waited patiently with the outhouse door cracked slightly. But as the minutes passed and the woman did not return, she began to worry. What happened to her outhouse messenger? Did she find Charlotte's bench mate?

Lord, please help this woman to hurry. I'm going to miss my train!

Finally, Charlotte breathed a sigh of relief when she saw the little woman making her way back as fast as her legs would carry her. Charlotte searched the woman's hands for her carpet bag, but they were empty.

Her helper came to an abrupt stop inches from the outhouse door. "I'm so sorry, Miss. I couldn't find her. No woman matching your description was waiting on any benches. Is there something else I can do to help?"

"No," Charlotte said morosely. "Thank you. You have been very kind. By any chance, did you see if the train leaving for Texas was still at the depot?"

"Oh, yes! But you must hurry! The conductor was just taking on the last passenger."

Charlotte had no time to waste. She had to be on that train to Texas. Her fiancé was waiting for her! And Charlotte possessed very little money in which to purchase another ticket.

She shut the door one last time. Eyeing the carpet bag, Charlotte made up her mind. She was sure the wealthy woman would not carry a sewing kit in her bag, but perhaps Charlotte could find something else of use to help mend her dress.

Charlotte opened the bag, noting the fine silks and satins of the undergarments. Charlotte's own nightclothes were a sturdy, serviceable cotton. Her bench mate's were incredibly soft and lush. Charlotte wondered wistfully what it would be like to wear such finery.

"No, time for that!" Charlotte reprimanded herself. "You've got to fix your dress and make your train."

Charlotte searched the bag for a pin, or a needle and thread, but there was nothing of the sort. Instead, there was a book of poetry, oh, wait! Some embroidery thread and a needle. No, too short, won't work. Charlotte tossed them back into the bag. Her movements were growing more frantic now.

As much as she hated to, she was going to need to borrow this woman's clothing so that she could get out of this outhouse.

Another knock sounded.

"Ye dead in there or somethin'?"

"No, quite alive. Out in a moment!" Charlotte called. A train whistle sounded. Her fingers flew, no longer caring that her dress was ending up in a heap on the dirt floor of an outhouse. Seriously, could her luck be any worse?

Charlotte dragged a white blouse over her head, followed by a gold skirt with a bustle that was firmly attached. Praise the Lord! A matching brocade belt completed her ensemble.

Without a second thought, Charlotte ran from the outhouse, her torn dress wadded up under her one arm and her borrowed carpet bag in the other.

She reached the platform where she had left the woman, just as the final train cars pulled away from the station. Amid the hissing steam and smoke, the train blew its whistle one last, mournful time.

Charlotte Mason, mail order bride from Atlanta, Georgia, had just missed her train.

IF you enjoyed *Bride of Pretense* by Cami Wesley and Amanda Tru, be sure to check these additional titles which are sure to please.

The Brides by Mail Series by Cami Wesley andAmanda Tru:
>Book 1: Bride of Pretense
>
>Book 2: Bride by Request (coming soon)

The Tru Exceptions Series by Amanda Tru:
>Book 1: Baggage Claim
>
>Book 2: Point of Origin
>
>Book 3: Mirage

Stand-Alone Novels by Amanda Tru:
>Secret Santa
>
>The Romance of the Sugar Plum Fairy
>
>Random Acts of Cupid
>
>The Assumption of Guilt

Proudly published by *Walker Hammond Publishers.*

Discussion Questions

ARE you an Addie or a Charlotte? We, the authors, regretfully admit that we are both more like Addie than Charlotte. Figuring out God's will for our lives is one of those questions we have both long questioned, marveling at the Charlottes who always seem to just know what God wants them to do.

What about you? As you read this book, were you able to relate to Addie and Charlotte? Can you recognize God's voice and direction in your own life?

We've come to believe that it's okay not to be a Charlotte. That sometimes, no matter what you do, it's going to *feel* like your prayers don't reach past the ceiling. Our prayer for you, however, is that you hold fast to your faith in those times when God seems silent, that you learn to recognize His voice when He speaks in a whisper, and that you completely depend on His Word as your guide.

May this book and the following questions cause you to reflect on your own life and better recognize His work and direction, blessing your relationship with God. May He draw you closer to Him, let you hear His voice, and grant you faith to walk in his will.

As the authors, we drew on some of our own experiences for Addie's character and the events of the book. Not that we've ever tried to wrestle a chicken. But we have burnt the bacon (repeatedly), and seem to have an amazing knack for having bizarre, and yet rather amusing, events lap at our heels! We only hope that they contain lessons that we learn from!

Throughout the book, numerous amusing events happen to Addie as she makes mistakes, learns from them, and develops a stronger faith in God and His providence.

1. What was your favorite part of the book?

2. How did this part add to Addie's character or teach her something?

   Psalm 37:23, Psalm 46:1

In many ways, Addie and Charlotte are opposites. Charlotte can cook. Addie can't. Addie is wealthy, Charlotte is poor. But even in spiritual matters, they are different. Addie is actually annoyed because Charlotte seems to have everything figured out, while she struggles to hear God and know His will.

3. Are you a Charlotte or an Addie? Do you hear from God clearly and find determining His will to be obvious, or do you struggle to even locate the path and wonder if God is on mute!

   Romans 8:26-27, 1 Thessolonians 5:16-19, Hebrews 10:36

It's easy to feel close to God when your prayers are being answered, but there are some times in life when you struggle to discern up from down, let alone trying to determine God's will!

4. Addie says that she feels like her prayer don't reach past the ceiling. Have you ever felt this way?

5. How did you deal with God's apparent silence?

6. Biblically, what do you think you should do when God seems silent?

   Proverbs 3:5-6, Isaiah 55:6, Psalm 34:17, Psalm 66:17-20

At the beginning of the book, Addie posed a question about determining God's will; however, that question wasn't answered until Charlotte arrived at the end of the book.

7. When Charlotte arrives, she says that sometimes God speaks in an urging that you can't shake. Addie realizes that her urge to check on Clementine might have been God speaking to her. When and how has God spoken clearly in your life or the lives of others?

8. Have you ever desperately needed to hear from God? Did He speak or seem to remain silent? What happened? Was your faith still able to grow through testing?

   James 1:12, James 1:2-4, Psalm 83:1

9. In Chapter 10, Charlotte finally answers Addie's question of how she determines God's will. Did you find her answer Biblical and accurate?

10. How do *you* determine God's will for your life?

    Philippians 4:6-7, Psalm 119:105, James 1:5

Forgiveness is another theme in this book. Charlotte quickly and easily forgives Addie, and yet Pete never forgave in time to reconcile with his brother.

11. Are you more like Charlotte, quick to forgive, or like Pete, where it takes long time to get past the hurt and reach forgiveness.

12. Have you ever felt or seen the consequences of unforgiveness?

    Ephesians 4:26, Matthew 6:14-15 Matthew 8:21-22, Luke 17:3-4

13. Have you ever felt or seen the blessings of forgiveness?

   Colossians 3:13, 1 Corinthians 13:4-6, Luke 6:37

In the end, Charlotte and Addie seem to both believe that everything happens for a reason, and that God had planned their lives, even with their mistakes.

14. Looking back on your life, can you see any instances where God arranged events and maybe even used your mistakes, to take you where He wanted you to be?

   Romans 8:28, Psalm 139:16, Jeremiah 29:11

While we wanted to write a meaningful book, we also wanted to write a story that was enjoyable, even amusing. So much of life is difficult that we wanted to provide a ray of sunshine, even an escape, for readers. To make a bright spot in an often dreary place.

15. Before you close in prayer, can you please share other "bright spots?" What is something that has blessed you or made you happy recently? What is something that made you smile?

Psalm 118:24, Psalm 126:2, Psalm 97:11-12, Proverbs 15:13

NOTES:

_____

_____

_____

_____

_____

_____

_____

_____

YESTERDAY SERIES

ALL six thrilling tales of time-travel in Amanda Tru's best-selling saga, the *Yesterday Series*, are available now in newly edited editions, complete with discussion questions for individuals or book clubs and all new timeline diagrams.

The Yesterday Series:

Book 1: Yesterday

Book 2: The Locket

Book 3: Today

Book 4: The Choice

Book 5: Tomorrow

Book 6: The Promise

ENJOY this sneak peek into *Yesterday*, available now wherever fine books are sold.

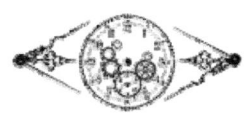

RED flashed against the bright white of the snow.

I slammed on the brakes. The SUV skidded toward the

guardrail.

My heart seemed to stop. I couldn't breathe. My body felt suspended as the mountainous terrain whirled across my vision. I braced for impact. Unexpectedly, the vehicle lurched as the tires found traction and came to a sudden stop

I sucked in air. My eyes frantically searched the heavy snowfall.

What had I seen?

Was it human?

Had I hit something?

The Sierra mountains were shrouded in the stillness of the winter storm, silent and revealing no secrets. Had I just imagined something dart in front of me?

I caught a glimpse of a fist out of the corner of my eye. I jumped. A strangled scream escaped my throat as the fist started hammering on my window. Heart thumping, I peered beyond the relentless pounding to see the outline of a woman in a red parka. She was screaming, but I couldn't understand her words.

Fingers fumbling and shaking, I rolled down my window. At her appearance, an electric current of shock ripped through me.

Blood streamed from somewhere on her head. It trickled down to her chin, leaving a dark red trail. Dirty tears streaked her cheeks, and her hair hung in clumps of frizzy knots.

I frantically jerked open my door.

"Are you okay?" I asked.

But she didn't answer. Instead, she continued to scream,

her hysterical cries now slicing through me.

"Help! Help! Please help me! I can't get them out!"

What was she talking about? My eyes traced an invisible line to where she was gesturing. A few yards in front of my own fender, the meager guardrail was bent and scraped. Peering through the falling snow, I could see beyond that to where the frozen earth had been torn up. Standing on the frame of my car door, I looked into the embankment off the side. Red tail lights glowed like beacons.

The shock to my senses was like a physical blow. I sprang out of the car, stepping into a blood stained patch of snow. Blood had dripped from the woman's leg where her torn pants exposed a jagged wound. Her sobbing and frantic cries continued, but she wasn't making sense.

Her skin was chalky green. She was in shock, yet I felt paralyzed. My medical background consisted of a three hour CPR and first aid class I'd taken over a year ago. Panic washed over me like a wave. I didn't know how to help her!

Desperate, I gently pushed her toward the back seat of the SUV. Her feet shuffled forward two steps, and then she collapsed. I caught her around the shoulders and practically dragged her rag doll frame to the back seat.

She roused enough to help as I lifted her into the back seat. I unraveled the scarf from my neck and wrapped it around her leg above the bloody gash, tying it as tightly as I could.

Reaching into the back of the SUV, I located a large flashlight and my old coat that I used when skiing. I wrapped the arms of the coat loosely around her leg, hoping the bulky material would soak up some of the blood.

"What's your name?" I asked the woman.

She cleared her throat and shook her head, her brow creasing with confusion. Instead, she began a new litany of faint but frantic cries about her family.

"You can tell me later. I'm Hannah."

"Help! My family… !"

"I'm going down into the ravine right now. Stay here. I'll help them. I promise."

Hoping I didn't just make a promise I couldn't keep, I shut the door and tripped my way through the snowdrifts toward the red haloed taillights.

I pulled my phone out of my coat pocket. There usually wasn't cell phone coverage on this road. But, just maybe…

No service.

This wasn't supposed to be happening! I should be at my sister's lodge at the top of the mountain not crawling down a steep embankment to help accident victims!

It wasn't even supposed to be snowing! I'd checked the weather report at least a dozen times: no new snow for the next week. Now it was practically a blizzard!

I took deep breaths, trying to control the panic and adrenaline running through my veins as I half climbed, half slid down the incline. This wasn't me. I'm not the brave sort. In fact, I'm pretty much a wimp!

I was facing the risk of a serious panic attack even before any of this had happened. The rational part of my brain said my fear was ridiculous. The roads were supposed to be clear. I'd driven to Silver Springs many times before. And, I was driving the biggest, meanest, previously-owned SUV an over-protective father could buy for his college-age daughter. Despite my best rationale, my hands were sweating, my heart was beating erratically, and I was still at the bottom of the mountain.

But those symptoms were nothing compared to what I experienced now. When my eyes collided with the blue sedan at the bottom, I wanted to turn around and run. The front of the car was wrapped around a tree. How could anyone survive an accident like this?

The gas station attendant's ramblings from earlier replayed in my head like a bad movie. Something about a tragic accident on this same road five years ago. The family had all died.

Taking a deep breath, I felt renewed determination run through my veins as it hitched a ride on an abundance of adrenaline. I had to do this.

"Hello, can anyone hear me?" I called as I slid the last few feet to the bottom of the ravine. My wrist scraped over some exposed branches on the way down, but the pain didn't register. I called again, louder.

No answer.

I didn't want to do this! I didn't want to see the scene inside the mangled car. I drew in a shaky, hiccuping breath.

Reaching the driver's side door, I shined the flashlight inside. The beam flickered in my shaking hand. I counted three passengers, motionless and unresponsive to the bright light. My stomach flipped as the beam caught blood marring each pale face.

I bent over, hyperventilating and gasping for breath. I couldn't do this! They were probably already dead! I closed my eyes. "Please, God, I can't do this! Help me!"

I released my breath slowly, then quickly swung my flashlight back inside before I lost my nerve.

About the Authors

Amanda Tru and **Cami Wesley** are sisters, best friends, and a dynamic writing team! Growing up, Amanda and Cami fought over who got to read books first and dreamed of being authors.

Amanda got her start first, and is the author of more than fourteen books under her own name. Finally convincing her sister to write with her, they wrote *Bride of Pretense* together, never imagining how much fun it would be to mix history, humor, and their Christian faith to develop a unique story and write every scene together. They now believe the most fun way to write is together and feel they bring out the best in each other. Of course, making each other cry with laughter along the way is an added bonus!

Amanda is a busy mom of three young boys and lives in Idaho. Cami is an equally busy mom of two girls and a boy and lives in California.

Both get their writing done at night, sacrificing sleep and a clean house to write stories that let others have an excuse to get out of their own sleep and cleaning!

Connect Online

Author site:

http://amandatru.blogspot.com/

Newsletter email sign up:

http://eepurl.com/ZQdw9

Facebook:

https://www.facebook.com/amandatru.author

https://www.facebook.com/pages/Cami-Wesley/1468705350116056

Twitter:

https://twitter.com/TruAmanda

GooglePlus+:

https://plus.google.com/+AmandaTru

Pinterest:

http://www.pinterest.com/truamanda/

Goodreads:

https://www.goodreads.com/author/show/5374686.Amanda_Tru